Rouge Numbered Week

Gary Celdom Case Journals

By

Douglas J. McLeod

Rouge Numbered Week

Gary Celdom Case Journals

Copyright © Douglas J. McLeod, 2014

McLeod, Douglas J. 1971 -

Rouge Numbered Week

ISBN-13: 978-0993773211

ISBN: 0-99377-321-4

1.   Detective – Fiction. 2. Toronto (Ont.) – Fiction.

I. Title.

Cover photograph: "Statue touchdown cfhof" by Alan Walker - My own work, ref: C191339. Licensed under Creative Commons Attribution-Share Alike 2.5 via Wikimedia Commons - http://commons.wikimedia.org/wiki/File:Statue_touchdown_cfhof.jpg#mediaviewer/File:Statue_touchdown_cfhof.jpg, and "Blood stain" by Panapp - Own work. Licensed under Creative Commons Attribution-Share Alike 3.0 via Wikimedia Commons - http://commons.wikimedia.org/wiki/File:Blood_stain.png#mediaviewer/File:Blood_stain.png

This book is set in Times New Roman

10 9 8 7 6 5 4 3 2 1

Acknowledgments

This book would not be possible without the support of some wonderful people in my life.

First, I want to thank my loving fiancée, Catherine. You are everything to me, and I want to thank you for helping me through this process.

Second, my family; especially, my aunt Patti, and my late great aunt, Pat. You two have been my biggest supporters, and I thank you both from the bottom of my heart.

Next, my fellow writing crazies I've met over the years: Jen F., Bethlyn, Cassandra, Christa, Jen H., Linda, Shaynie, Elissa, Mary, Jessie, and countless others whom I've forgotten. You lot are the craziest people I've ever met, and I consider you all fellow compatriots along for this wild ride.

And finally, I dedicate this book to all of the fans of Canadian football. I've been a fan of the sport for 35 years, and I wanted to say thank you for supporting this great game. We've had our ups and downs, but after 102 years, we continue to thrive. It's true what they say, "Our balls are bigger," and I've got a huge pair of grapefruits to put this one out.

CHAPTER 1

If there is one time of the year I have mixed emotions about, it's the month of November. There is a distinct nip in the air. Overcast days can bring anything from a bone chilling rain that freezes on the ground upon contact, to a feverous snowfall. The malls have swung into full Christmas shopping sales; although, in my opinion, the holiday sale season doesn't get underway until the annual Santa Claus Parade has taken place. And for the eclectic few that I have come to know three years prior, they are within the throes of creative abandon as they toil away at their keyboards in an attempt to hammer out a fifty thousand word novel within the span of thirty days. While, I confess that I still attempt the challenge in the years since I had been introduced to the aforementioned motley crew, my days lately have been spent behind my desk; writing up reports on whatever case I have been working on, or pounding the pavement with my partner/girlfriend. On this particular day, I happened to be toiling more on the former.

My professional -- and personal -- colleague and I had recently been finishing up a case where we rounded up a couple of hoodlums responsible for some thefts in the St. Lawrence Market area. While I admit there are some interesting wares that could be stolen from the rustic shopping complex, I rarely saw the appeal for some black market grocery items. Logic would have dictated the thieves would have targeted the art gallery in the upstairs portion, but our investigation uncovered that the culprits were working their way up to it; using the deli meats and cheeses as a ruse to throw us off the trail before they hit the big ticket items. Thankfully, we were able to arrest the sets of sticky fingers before any assets of notable value were lost.

Now, I was stuck behind my desk, filling out my reports on the matter. I've really had to clean up my work ever since I was on the brink of losing my job of the past 27 years a couple of months ago. Apparently, my superiors

1

and the fine detectives with the Special Investigations Unit did not take too kindly to the manner I captured a trio of break-and-enter artists; who also had weapons and drug offences attached to their rap sheets. Granted, I do confess to the fact I didn't inform the proper departments beforehand when my partner, a couple of Constables, and myself stormed their dwelling in Regent Park to arrest the scum. For that lapse of procedure, I had been suspended for two weeks. It was the wake-up call I needed because I had lost my rational judgment in recent years. I had heard it from all angles after I was called out onto the carpet: the S.I.U. detectives, my superior officer, my partner, and the worst of them all... the spirit of my dearly departed fiancée.

So, here I was, doing the necessarily procedural duties. I was so engrossed in filling out my report that I didn't notice my partner, Detective Jessica Amerson walk by my desk, with the aforementioned spectre in tow with her.

"Please tell me you're not working on your novel writing project, Celdom," Jessica cautioned.

"Negative, Amerson," I assured. "I'm just finishing up the reports on the St. Lawrence Market bust."

"A likely story, Gary," the spirit of Karen Prairie scolded. "You're probably jotting down some plot notes just before we came in."

"Look for yourself," I challenged. "I highly doubt people would write a novel where a stolen block of Havarti and a kielbasa was a focal point in the narrative."

"Gary," the ghost countered, "this is the same event where people discuss urinal cakes and free shrimp dinners in their exploits. Deli items can't be that far off."

My partner looked over my shoulder and confirmed, "He's speaking the truth this time, Karen. I can see he's using the proper forms for this."

"And why wouldn't I?" I chuffed. "Do you two think I want another suspension without pay after Detectives Johnson and Dyakowski from the S.I.U. reprimanded me over the Saunders arrest back in September?"

"Well, no," my girlfriend attempted to reason, "but, I know how wrapped up you get sometimes during the novel writing challenge when November rolls around."

I sighed with exasperation. "Jessica, Karen, I've skated on thin ice *way* too often in recent years. I don't want to risk crashing through the surface and throwing away a long career in the process."

The spirit mocked, "So, the changed Gary Celdom act is still going on. I'm surprised you've been able to keep it up for this long."

"As am I," Jessica added. "I would've thought you would've been called out on the carpet by Lt. Davies or someone higher up on the food chain by now."

Had I been my old self I would have blown up at the two females before me; however, I gritted my teeth and took their doubt with a grain of salt. Given the history I've had, I don't blame them for giving me the gears. I had been beating myself up ever since the suspension for a fortnight, and Jessica and Karen have never let me forget about it. I guess it was their way of testing my mettle to see if there were any chinks in my newly formed armor. I had been good so far, but I could understand why they would be so skeptical after all this time.

I shook my head, "I see what you two are doing, and while I do commend you for your effort, it's not going to work. Besides, I can't really let my frustrations show. Remember, Amerson, if I'm cut loose, you're going to have to start working with someone else on the beat. Do you really want to endure working with someone who might not be as tolerable as I am?"

Jessica began to backtrack over my suggestion. She liked working with me, and it was because of the rapport she and I shared we had developed the romantic relationship outside of work the previous August when I was caught in the midst of a hostage standoff at a fan convention in Yorkville.

If I was not around on a daily basis, that foundation we had established might have begun to deteriorate, and it was not something she wanted to risk throwing away; not after she had harbored such deep-rooted feelings for a while.

M partner retracted, "I apologize, Gary. You know I only grill you because I care about you, as does Karen. I do have to commend you for the progress you've made so far in cleaning up your act. I can imagine it hasn't been easy for you to make this change."

I chuckled, "It has been quite an adjustment, I do admit. However, I am committed to working here for at least a few years more. You're not going to get rid of me that easily."

Jessica smiled, "I'm relieved to hear that. I don't want you to leave anytime soon. Besides, like you said, there are a couple of things on your career 'bucket list' you want to cross off before you hang it up."

Karen chimed in, "The main one I'm still waiting to happen after 20 years."

I turned to the spectre, "And like I've told you before, I need to overcome the psychological and emotional block I have within my psyche before I can do that."

"At least you have Knoblach to help you through that," Jessica cited.

I nodded, "Believe me, I am very thankful Lt. Davies assigned me to see her regularly over the past three years. My sessions with her have really helped."

Ever since the aftermath of a difficult case where my previous romantic interest ended her long-distance relationship with me, my superior officer felt I was not in the right emotional mind to be an effective member of the Toronto P.D. Fortunately for me, Lt. John Davies saw there was still a solid detective residing within me, so he suggested I start seeing the police psychologist, Ann Knoblach, in a bid for me to get my id under control. It would be during my one-on-one sessions with her where I was able to get to the root of my problems: I had not been able to overcome the psychological and emotional trauma I experienced two decades ago when Karen was assassinated right before me on our wedding day. It was a traumatic experience I had never been able to let go of, and it is because of that, I continued to see and have conversations with her ghostly spirit in the years since the tragedy. I'm fortunate I now have Jessica, who could empathize with the inner turmoil I have endured all of these years. My partner knew of my plight and the difficulties I had on a daily basis ever since Lt. Davies assigned us to each other two years ago; however, Detective Amerson did not really grasp the full scope of it until Karen revealed herself to my now girlfriend during the hostage siege three months ago. What's more, in a move that shocked both Jessica and yours truly, the spirit gave her blessing for us to enter into a personal relationship outside of the confines of our workplace. It was a new dynamic the two of us had since embraced, and we were thankful Karen had stuck around to be a good friend and guide throughout the weeks since.

After a little bit more banter, Lt. Davies came out of his office and called out to us, "Amerson, Celdom, in my office now."

"Uh oh," Karen worried, "looks like you two are in hot water over something."

"Don't be too sure of that," I deflected. "It might be to talk about this robbery case."

Jessica gave me a wry grin, "Shall we, partner?"

"I believe we shall." I smiled, then turned to Karen, "Excuse us, please."

My partner and I made our way to our superior's office and closed the door behind us.

~ * * * ~

Jessica asked, "You wanted to see us, Lieutenant?"

Lt. Davies was a man in his late 40s. He had been assigned to our Division 10 years ago after the retirement of Lesley Polanski who had really given me a rough time under her tenure. I can't say I blamed her, though. Back then, I was the type of detective who would make her rip her hair out over my recklessness, and she made sure I heard about it. When Lt. Davies took over, he was more understanding of my foibles; however, my antics started to wear thin on him over the years. It had been a Division legend that the grey hairs on his head were attributed to having to deal with me during the past decade. I'll admit I haven't been the easiest detective to tolerate, but at least he was willing to put up with me. It was thanks to him that I had the support circle in Jessica and Dr. Knoblach, and why I haven't been told to turn in my badge and hang it up after 27 years of service.

Lt. Davies leaned forward in his chair, and clasped his hands on top of his desk. "Yes, Detectives. We just got a report over the wire that there have been a couple of bodies found on the university campus near Hoskin and Devonshire. I want you and Celdom to go help in the investigation."

"Are they students on the campus?" I quizzed.

"That's undetermined at the current juncture. That's why I want you two to check it out and see what you can turn up."

"We're on it, sir," Jessica assured, as we turned to leave his office.

"Finally, some action," I commented, as we walked towards our desks to grab our coats. "It's been a while since we've worked on a homicide. I was beginning to get tired of all the petty thefts we've been dealing with lately."

"You and me, both," my partner added. "While it does get some bad guys off the street, I prefer the real glamour cases too."

What the two of us didn't expect is that these would be the first in a string of dead bodies that would turn up over the following week.

CHAPTER 2

When Jessica and I arrived at the crime scene 15 minutes later, the Forensics Unit was combing the area for possible evidence to the murders that had transpired. Parking on Devonshire was pretty limited due to the street's placement by the main stadium on the University's campus; although, there wasn't much of a facility now like it used to be decades ago. Back in the 1950s and 60s, Varsity Stadium housed many a college and pro football game. In fact, it was host to some of the most famous Canadian football championships in its storied history. The most notorious was the contest back in 1950 between Toronto and Winnipeg where the field became a mud pit. Lore has it there was a heavy snowfall that hit Toronto the day before the game. The grounds crew used heavy machinery to clear the field. Unfortunately, the equipment damaged the field severely; causing the sloppy conditions. The playing surface was in such terrible shape, legend says a player almost drowned in a puddle on the turf. The hometown side would win the contest by a score of 13-0; however, there have been other championship games played in equally adverse weather conditions over the years – just not at Varsity.

That being said, I was disappointed when they tore the stadium down and rebuilt the facility anew. I understood they did it because the infrastructure was crumbling; however, I didn't care for how they remodelled it afterwards. Gone was the natural grass surface, in favour for the modern day artificial turf some sporting teams prefer; that much I could accept. What disheartened me was the fact that when they rebuilt the stands, they only constructed them on one side of the field instead of a traditional bowl shape. While I know the university's football team has lost its lustre to more popular programs at the schools in London, Guelph, Kingston, and Hamilton, I thought the refurbished stadium had sacrificed some of its legacy by not attempting to recreate its hallowed stands of yore. At least the neighbouring arena for the school's hockey teams had remained standing throughout the revitalization, but one had to wonder how long it would be before they decide to replace it with a new modern day ice pad of its own. Especially since a rival university in the city had recently converted the storied Maple Leaf Gardens into a new sports and recreational facility for its hockey, basketball, and volleyball programs. But, that was something I was trivializing over. I had a murder investigation I needed to look into.

My partner and I approached one of the members of the Forensics team, Tamara Hutchins, and attempted to get an update on the situation.

"Detectives Celdom and Amerson," she recognized. "Here to see what the streets drudged up today?"

"Pretty much, Hutchins," Jessica confirmed. "What have you got for us?"

"Two victims, one male and one female. Both of them appear to be in their late 20s."

"A little old to be university students, don't you think?" I posed.

"They could have been attending night classes on the campus," Jessica reasoned.

"A distinct possibility," Tamara explained, "but neither of them was carrying text books. My feeling was they were making their way from the coffee shop up at Bedford at Bloor to a destination along Harbord -- possibly a place of residence -- when they were attacked."

"Were they shot or stabbed?" I asked.

"Both victims appear to have suffered gunshot wounds to their torsos. Whoever killed them did it at point blank range."

"Possibly targeted," I supposed.

"Any particular motive," Jessica probed, "like a robbery gone bad?"

"It doesn't appear that way," Tamara noted. "We've checked both the victims' wallets for any identification, and it doesn't look like anything was removed from them."

"So, I'm assuming we've got an ID on the bodies then?" I pointed out.

"Actually, we do, Detective Celdom. The male is Brad Dawkins, and the woman is Paula Simmons."

"So, a boyfriend and girlfriend duo," Jessica presumed.

"Or a common law coupling if they have been living together in the same dwelling for a while," I countered. "There are some unions that go that route."

"An avenue I'm surprised you two haven't explored yet."

My partner rolled her eyes, and let out an exasperated sigh. "Is there anyone at the Division who doesn't know about Detective Celdom and me?"

"No, I think it is pretty much common knowledge to everyone who works there. I mean, come on. You two have been an item now for what, three months now?"

"Be it as it may," I interjected, albeit in an uncomfortable tone. "The common practice for a man and a woman to be defined as 'common law' is they have to have been living together for at least 12 months, and Detective Amerson and I have never discussed the concept of us residing under the same roof."

Tamara continued her interrogation, "While that may be true, is it something the two of you might explore sometime down the road?"

Man, was this woman being an inquisitive, yet nosy Parker. While I admit the line of questioning was unprofessional, given the circumstances of the environment we were in at the moment, I didn't mind it all that much. However, it was something that noticeably agitated my partner.

"Look, Hutchins," Jessica snapped. "This is neither the time, nor the place to be discussing such a sensitive and personal subject. So, unless you want to be reprimanded by your superiors, I suggest you cut this childish bullshit and stick to the two corpses underneath the tarps behind you. Do I make myself clear?"

The sternness and threatening tone in Detective Amerson's voice resonated with Tamara to the point where the Forensics investigator began to apologize profusely for her lack of professionalism.

"You're right, Detective Amerson. That was completely uncalled for by me. I'm so sorry."

"Well, if people around here quit feeding the God damn rumour mill, we'd all give more efficient service to the people that those asshats down at City Hall are always complaining for."

Damn, Jessica was really fired up. What Tamara had suggested must have really touched a nerve with her. However, like my partner, I was getting tired of all of the wagging tongues behind our backs because we happened to be dating. I felt it was taking away from everyone's effectiveness; yet, the two of us still trudged on, doing the best job we could possibly do on a daily basis. Now, if everyone else in the department could follow our lead, we'd all be a more cohesive unit. But, when she threw in the jab at our municipal politicians, I had to stifle a chuckle. It's no secret that I have disdain for the current crop of bureaucrats we have representing the City of Toronto. Then again, I don't particularly care for elected officials in general. However, after hearing Jessica slam the idiots down at the intersection of Queen and Bay, it made me wonder if some of my idiosyncrasies were starting to rub off on her.

"Alright, everyone," I attempted to defuse the situation. "I know we're all on edge here, given how the lines between professional and personal lives are being blurred. But, Detective Amerson does have a point. The main focus here should be on the two victims who lost their lives, and also trying to see if there is any evidence that could lead us to their killer. Ms. Hutchins, has your team been able to discover anything near the scene that could help us out in this investigation?"

"Unfortunately not," Tamara informed. "Whoever did these murders left the crime scene pretty clean."

"I see. So, no metal filings from the murder weapon that could have determined the distance from where the shots were fired before the bullets struck their targets?"

~ * * * ~

My partner had walked away from my interview to peruse the crime scene. Jessica decided to head over to the tarps where the murder victims were shrouded. She wanted to see if there was any particular reason why these two individuals were targeted. According to Hutchins' accounts, Dawkins and Simmons didn't have any of their personal possessions disturbed, so the possibility of it being a botched mugging was ruled out. To probe further, Jessica lifted the coverings to get a good look at the recently deceased. My partner ended up dismayed at the fact two young lives had been taken for no concrete reason. Dawkins was a stocky male, about 5'10" with sandy blonde hair and a chevron moustache. Simmons had a bit of weight on her, as well, but was formulated to accentuate her womanly attributes, and would have probably stood 5'5". The female member of the duo sported brunette hair that had been done in a stylish ponytail.

It appeared both victims were shot from head on, as it appeared the bullets pierced their chests, right where their hearts were. Whoever fired the fatal blasts must have been a superb marksman; however, depending on how close the range was, accuracy might not have been an issue. Jessica attempted to analyze the situation in her mind: where the shooter was positioned, what possible motive he – or she – might have had. Was it a matter of a jilted lover? Or something more inexcusable, like a homicidal nut that randomly fired a gun with no real rhyme or reason? It looked like my partner had no real answers either until something shining in the moonlight caught her eye. She decided to investigate further and noticed both victims possessed the same identical item.

"Celdom," Jessica called out to me, "could you come over here? I think I might have found something."

I excused myself from Ms. Hutchins and walked over to where my partner was crouching. "What have you got?" I enquired.

"Look at this," she pointed out. "Both of the victims are wearing similar pins on their jackets."

I peered closer to the blood spattered coats the recently deceased were cloaked in and noticed both of them wore lapel pins of a distinct shape. They looked like boats, but the vessel's shells were formed to look like a football. Also, protruding from the sides of those football shells, looked like very thin lines into a swath of light blue; almost as if they were oars immersed in an animated sheath of water.

"I recognize this," I announced. "This is the logo of the Boatmen."

Jessica looked at me confused. "The Boatmen? I thought their logo was a blue shield with a big 'B' in the centre."

"That's what they are now, but back in the 1980's, when they were still playing down at the Exhibition Grounds, this was what their logo looked like."

"Okay, so they're both football fans."

"Canadian football fans of the pro team here in Toronto, a rarity in its own right."

"Do you think these two were targeted by a rival supporter?"

"I find that unlikely. The Boatmen's main rival is the Hamilton Tiger-Cats, and I find it unlikely that someone from Hamilton would be traversing the streets near the university on a Thursday night."

"Umm, I don't want to alarm you, Celdom, but, Thursday night, at Hoskin and Devonshire – which isn't a kilometre from Spadina and College, and a possible Tiger-Cat fan suspect. Are you thinking what I'm thinking?"

I was taken aback by the conclusions my partner was presuming. "Oh no," I attempted to discount. "I know he has some issues, and his mental faculties aren't all there, but I highly doubt committing a double homicide would be something that would enter his mind."

Jessica reasoned, "Be it as it may, he's the only person that immediately springs to mind. I'm not saying he did. I know he's our friend and all, but we can't necessarily rule him out this early into the investigation."

I took a deep and concerted sigh, and suggested we walk to our vehicle, and commence the long drive to Scarborough. It was something I was dreading, and I sincerely hoped Jessica's hunch was incorrect this time around.

CHAPTER 3

I suggested to Jessica we should try the rehab facility on Russell Street before we made the long trek out to Scarborough in a bid to interview our first, and so far, only suspect in the double homicide. Much to our chagrin, by the time we got to the building on the university campus' southwestern quadrant, he had already left for home. Jessica thought I should attempt to contact him on his mobile phone, but he didn't have it turned on. It would make sense that he wouldn't; his phone was out-dated, so he wouldn't have been able to get a signal while underground on the subway. As Bloor Street bled into the Danforth over the Don Valley, I couldn't help but hang on to the notion that our friend would never result to such tactics. If anything, he would be more a target than a shooter, given the way he switched allegiances four years ago.

For over 25 years, he had been a staunch supporter of the local Boatmen; being a devout season ticket holder. He still remembers when he took the train out to Ottawa for the Championship Game back in 2004; sitting behind the opposing team's bench, and cheering the Double Blue to a 27-19 victory in front of 51,242 fans from across the country who had gathered in the Nation's Capital for the festivities. While he doesn't want to admit it, his prized possession is an autographed jersey by the Boatmen's most beloved personality; a player, who later coached that championship squad eight years ago in Ottawa, and is now a community ambassador to the team. However, his allegiances changed soon after the last time Toronto hosted the championship game back in 2007.

Basking in the glow of what was by far, one of the most popular championship game festivals of all-time – helped by the first ever match-up for the prized chalice of the Canadian professional gridiron between two long-standing Prairie rivals – came the announcement that naysayers called the death knell for the Canadian game which had a long-standing, rich heritage. A major telecommunications corporation, who now owns the city's iconic summer sports venue, announced a partnership with the nearest American football franchise down in Buffalo to bring a select few "home" dates to Toronto where they would be contested. While it was seen as a public relations move by the American club to broaden their fan base, purists of the Canadian game – like our friend – saw it as a slap in the face, and a great insult. He believed the Boatmen rolled over and allowed the big boys from across the Niagara River to lay claim to football superiority in the city. In a huff, the man who had loved the Boatmen for so long decided to, if you'll excuse the pun, 'abandon ship.' He would then turned his support to the Double Blue's long-standing rivals from down the Queen Elizabeth Way, where he had been attending games at the iconic Ivor Wynne Stadium for the past four seasons and parts of a fifth.

The one thing I wonder about him now is what he would be doing for his Canadian football fix when next June rolls around. The Tiger-Cats had announced they would be tearing down Ivor Wynne after the season ended and build a new facility on its grounds, with the intent of having it open for the start of the season in 2014. That left the issue of where the Black and Gold would be playing for their 2013 campaign. The original intent would have them playing on the grounds of Hamilton's university; however, the team and the school's Board of Governors weren't able to reach an agreement. This has forced the team to look elsewhere. The current front runner would be to temporarily relocate the club to the university down in London, Ontario for the season while the new stadium was being built in the Scott Park area of Hamilton. However, the club had not made an official announcement of where their 2013 home schedule will be played, but they have promised they will have first priority of seats wherever they do end up playing, as well as, first dibs on seats in the new stadium in 2014. Whether or not our friend would be making the treks to the temporary home next year was yet to be determined, but in all likelihood he would wait it out until the sparkling new facility opened in two years.

I decided to try our friend's cell phone one more time as we turned off Danforth Avenue onto Kingston Road. Fortunately for me, it rang through. He must have turned it on after he got off the subway.

"Hello," our friend answered, "Bennett here."

"Hey Phil," I responded with my novel writing challenge moniker, "It's Toronto Phoenix."

"Oh hello, Detective Celdom," he recognized. "How are you making out in this year's contest?"

"I've had to put it on hold due to an investigation that's currently ongoing. That's why I'm calling."

"Is there something wrong?" Phil's voice had a tone of concern.

"Possibly, Detective Amerson and I are on our way to your place right now. How far away are you from there?"

"I'm actually on the bus home right now. Tell you what. There's a coffee shop at the intersection of Eglinton and Cedar that should still be open. It's the first light east of Markham Road. We can meet each other there and discuss this."

"That would be greatly appreciated. We'll see you there."

"See you there in a few." Phil hung up his phone.

"So, what's the skinny?" Jessica asked.

"He's on his way home now. He's going to meet us at a coffee shop near his place."

"Will it still be open at this hour?"

"He says it should still be. We'll see how late it's open until when we get there, and if need be, we can walk back to his place and finish our interview there."

"Sounds like a reasonable plan."

The two of us turned off of Kingston onto Markham Road and made our way to the rendezvous point. As we approached the coffee shop, we seemed to be confused as to its entry point. There was an exit from the business' parking lot that led onto the westbound lanes of Eglinton, but there was no access to it from the eastbound side of the street. We turned onto the driveway for the plaza complex across the street, and were about to ask for directions when the bus Phil was on pulled up behind us. My friend recognized our vehicle and walked over to us.

"Good evening, Detectives," he greeted. "You guys made good time."

"Evening, Phil," I responded in kind. "Not to be so much of a bother, but how do we get into the parking lot of the coffee shop across the street?"

"Yeah, there doesn't appear to be a direct entrance from Eglinton into there," Jessica added.

"Oh, the entrance is off of Cedar. If you're driving eastbound, you have to turn left and it's the first driveway on the left-hand side."

"Thanks for the advisory."

"Since it's not that far," I suggested, "why don't you hop into the backseat and save you a short walk?"

"Much appreciated, Detective Celdom." Phil climbed in.

~ * * * ~

After a drive through the stoplight and a little navigation into the parking lot, the three of us entered the coffee shop. It turns out this particular location was open for another couple of hours, so it allowed us a reasonable amount of time to discuss the situation at hand. We ordered our coffee and proceeded over to a four-seated table in the corner of the shop where the interview began soon after.

"So, what's so pressing that you two had to drive all the way to Scarborough to talk to me?" Phil asked.

"We received a call that there was a double homicide near the stadium at the main university campus," I informed.

"That's terrible." Phil sounded disheartened. "Were they students at the university?"

17

Jessica chimed in, "No, they were older than the normal university student; we figure in their late 20s."

"I'm sorry to hear that."

Jessica continued, "But, here's the thing: both of the victims were wearing 1980s era Boatmen pins."

A befuddled look formed on Phil's face. "Were they actual logo pins, or were they from their fan club?"

I blinked, "There's a difference?"

Phil explained, "I used to be a member of their fan club back in 1995. I even went on a road trip with them to Baltimore to attend a game because that was back during those lame American expansion years. Anyway, the fan club's logo is similar to that of the old 'boat' logo. The difference is, on the boat's sail it will have the name of the fan club printed on it; whereas, the actual vintage logo has a simple 'B' on the sail."

I turned to my partner and gave her a look, asking her, "Was it an actual team pin or a fan club trinket?"

She returned with a look of her own. "I can't remember for certain, but another look at their clothes once we get to the Coroner's Office will tell us for sure."

Phil asked, "But, that aside, what does that have to do with me?"

Now, I was in a delicate bind. How do you ask a friend you've known for a few years if he was somehow responsible in the deaths of two individuals without offending him? It's something that needed to be done with the utmost of tact, but it was damn near impossible to execute effectively.

I took a sip of my coffee, and I attempted to get the words out. "Well, I don't know how to say this," I stammered.

"We don't mean to offend," Jessica cautiously chose her words, "but, given the rivalry history between the Boatmen and the Ti-Cats, and the knowledge that you happened to be in the general vicinity…"

"Whoa, whoa, whoa," Phil interrupted. "Let me get this straight. You think that because I'm now a supporter of the Double Blue's main rival, I would resort to such a heinous act?"

"We're not saying you did," Jessica defended.

"It's just something we need to explore given the circumstances," I explained.

I was expecting Phil to blow his top and tear a strip off of both of us, but much to my surprise, he was calm when offering his defence.

He took a deep breath. "Now, Detectives, I can understand why you might have thought of this, and I don't fault you for doing so; you're just doing your job. However, while I do confess that I have switched allegiances, I offer no ill will to any member of 'Boatmen Nation'; whether it may be its players, personnel, front office, or even their fans. I find them to be fellow kin in the grander family of Canadian football fans. Now, I can't say the same for rival factions in other parts of the league -- like between Calgary and Edmonton, or even Saskatchewan and Winnipeg – but I like to think that we're one big sports nation collective who wants to see the sport thrive and flourish. Hell, I'm even looking forward to the league's eventual return to Ottawa in a couple years' time. In my opinion, the only people who want to see the league wiped out are the media types who believe the American game is the only "true" brand of football out there. But even then, they would have a hard time competing for sports dollars with the major league hockey team, but it's been like that for years in this city. However, despite my views, I assure you. I was nowhere near the stadium at the university."

"You're positively sure of that?" Jessica asked.

"Unless you count riding the Bloor-Danforth subway over to Spadina and then catching the 510 replacement buses down to College for my group therapy tonight as 'being in the area'. But, that's purely by coincidence. The problem gambling unit is the only one they haven't moved over to the new facilities down at Queen and Ossington."

I tried to change the line of questioning. "Speaking of which, how is the therapy coming along? I haven't heard any status updates about your addiction recovery since we saw you thrown out of Greenwood a couple of months ago."

"It's been difficult," Phil admitted. "It doesn't help matters that there's this one guy in the group who is on more shaky ground than I am; always being tempted to go up to Woodbine to play the ponies, or up to Rama to hit the blackjack tables. You'd think he would have better resolve, yet he always ends up at those places and gambles whatever little cash he has away."

Jessica said, "That must be really difficult to hear; especially, when you're on shaky ground yourself."

"Believe me, Detective Amerson, it is. I've done alright so far; however, hearing him regale of his problems does give me urges. The thing is, since I can't go to the track or the casino anymore, that only leaves the lottery retailers, and they're practically everywhere. Sure, I'm usually good, and I only stop by the one at the grocery store to buy bus tokens. However, when I hear that 'Winner's Chime' part of me gets the thought, 'maybe if I buy just one lotto ticket or one scratch-and-win, I can limit myself, and I'll be fine.' But, the fact of the matter is, if I buy one, it'll just lead to another, and another, and then I'll just be feeding my destructive addiction over and over again. That's a road I really don't want to go back down again."

"I know it's not easy," I remarked, "considering the province is so 'in your face' with their advertising; whether it be a big weekly lotto jackpot, a new daily game, or even enticing you to go to a casino."

"Oh, I need to tell you about this one I saw the other day that I thought was a complete insult to those who are emotionally fragile." Phil replied.

"What was it about?" I probed.

"It was one for the big casino resort down in Niagara Falls, on the Canadian side," he described. "It featured a couple at a restaurant, having a nice casual dinner date. The guy says that he enjoys spending time with her and all, and then the woman says that she has something to tell him. She waves the serving staff over, and does the whole cheesy birthday cake presentation bit. But, the difference is, the cake and the song the staff is singing is basically to tell the guy that she's dumping him. The commercial ends with the caption, 'Need some fun?' before placing the casino resort's logo."

Jessica cringed. "Ouch! That's a funny commercial, but I agree, it is quite insensitive."

"How so?" I asked my partner.

"Think about it, Gary. The advertisers are going for the angle where the guy has been told that his happy relationship is now over. He's going to be upset and depressed. So, why not come gamble at our facilities and forget your troubles. They're completely going for the emotionally distraught gambling demographic."

"And one thing they teach you in problem gambling therapy is not to gamble when you're in the wrong frame of mind," Phil added. "When you do so, you end up gambling more than you initially intend to, and for the most part, end up losing more than you win. Yes, gambling will get your mind off of it temporarily, but in the long run, it will end up causing more problems than what you had to begin with."

I commended my friend, "Well, that's good that you're able to recognize such a trigger. At least now, you know the warning signs before you actually go through with it."

"Recognizing has never been my problem, Detective Celdom. My issue is the odd lapse of judgment where I know such behaviour is wrong, but I still go ahead and do it anyway. It's the thrill and rush that I miss more than anything, and that's due to the need of a certain brain chemical that I crave. Sure, I can drink all of the coffee I want to get a decent level of caffeine so it could be a placebo to the sensation, but it's just not the same.

I mean, I know my brain has not been in the right balance for years; that's why I've been on prescriptions for my mental health issues since I was a kid. However, this is just another facet of why I seem so messed up."

"Well, regardless, you seem to have been doing right so far. Plus, your mind's not a complete waste. Every November you try to write a 50,000-word novel in 30 days, so that takes some mental and creative talent."

"That reminds me," Jessica asked, "how are you faring so far this year? I remember you were interviewing Detective Celdom a few weeks back as research for your latest project."

"It's coming along alright. I'm just a little over halfway to the 50K, and I'm hoping to log a few more words this weekend. One of the big events of the local chapter is taking place."

"Is the Overnighter this weekend?" I asked.

"No, they decided to push that to the final weekend of the month this year. This one is the big write-in on the subway."

I nodded, "That's usually a fun event. You guys ride the Yonge-University-Spadina line from one end to the other and back again; all while working away on your respective novels. You should be able to log quite a few words this year, now that you have your Netbook."

"It will definitely be an asset when I'm away from home at these writing sessions. My main goal is to log a plethora at the Overnighter. Sure, I usually get at least 5,000 words during that one night when I scribble them out by hand, but with the benefit of having an actual keyboard to type things out, I'm sure to blow that mark right out of the water."

"Well, hopefully you'll be successful this time around."

"Could we give you a ride home?" Jessica asked. "It's the least we could do after putting you on the spot like this."

"I appreciate the offer, Detective Amerson, but it's not really all that far to my apartment building from here, so I'm going to walk home. Besides, after doing a fair bit of sitting since I left my apartment for group earlier today, my legs need the exercise."

The three of us parted company with Phil walking down the sidewalk to a couple of driveways away, then turning in towards a block of four apartment buildings that stood behind the strip mall shadowing the coffee shop. I really hated to have accused him of the slayings at the university since he's had so many issues to deal with already; however, this is part of our job, and this early into the investigation we have to look at all the possibilities before narrowing things down to the correct solution.

~ * * * ~

Jessica noticed I was feeling a little off when we left the coffee shop. She asked as we entered our vehicle, "Are you alright there, Celdom?"

"Yeah, I'll be okay," I assured. "I feel guilty for having to interview Bennett over this."

"I know you do, but we can't rule anything out at the present juncture. If we leave any stones unturned, this could come back and bite our asses, and you've been treading on thin ice lately."

"That I have, and I appreciate the concern. Especially since there might be a possibility that if I go down, I might inadvertently drag you down with me, and I don't want that to happen. You have a long career ahead of you, while I'm nearing the end of the line on mine."

Jessica patted my hand, "Don't worry, Gary. I'm going to make sure we do this the proper way."

"Do you think after his speech we can rule out Bennett for the rest of the case?"

"Honestly, I'm not sure." Jessica sighed, as she shifted the car into gear and pulled out of the parking lot onto Eglinton. "For the time being, we have to take him for his word. But, until we get some more concrete data from Tamara and the rest of the Forensics team, we have to put him in the Suspect Archive for now."

That was a possibility I did not want to have to admit, but my partner was correct. One of my close friends might be a murderer, and it was a notion that tore at me.

CHAPTER 4

After finishing my shift down at the Division – which involved doing some paperwork regarding the Dawkins and Simmons murders – I headed back to my little bungalow in East York to try and get some sleep. I was still in shock over the remote possibility that Phil could have been responsible for their slayings. I believed what he told me at the Scarborough coffee shop, but there was still the minute notion that he could have snapped and killed two people. No, I couldn't think like that. Bennett might have had some issues over the years, but he couldn't be compelled to fatally harm anyone.

Even then, the method of the killings on the university campus: fatal gunshot wounds. He wouldn't have gone out and bought a firearm to "bust a cap" in anyone, would he? Sure, if he was provoked, he might, but Bennett seemed more the type of person who would resort to a verbal assault instead of physical violence. I believed he would have had a lot more civility than to raise his fist, or a weapon at anyone. My head was still trying to weigh all of the thoughts and doubts of the situation. I walked through the door of my house where my pet husky, Benny, greeted me. However, his cheerful mood couldn't break my confused state. All I could do was drop my keys off in their usual resting place, walk into my living room, and collapse into my recliner; still trying to piece everything together.

Benny, the endearing animal that he is, walked over to me and rested his head in my lap. He looked up at me as to ask, "What's wrong, Dad?" I scratched behind his ear and began to tell him my dilemma.

"I'm sorry, Benny," I said. "I can't help but think about a bombshell that was dropped onto me tonight regarding your 'brother.' I don't think he did anything, but the remote inkling that he might have is a shock to my system."

The husky's ears perked up when I mentioned Phil. The two had the pleasure of meeting each other during the Charity Auction at the last *Northern Lights* convention once everything settled down after the hostage situation, and immediately hit it off. Outside of Jessica and me, Phil was the person Benny adored the most. How could I tell the little guy that his third most favourite person was now a suspect for a possible double homicide? Would the husky turn on him, or would Benny become aggressive towards me or Jessica for accusing him as a guilty party? I was at a loss for words because I didn't want to plant a seed that could shatter the illusion of anyone to the pet I adore.

"I don't know what to say about it," I sighed. "I hope it's nothing as serious as what my psyche is thinking it is, but it's just the seed of doubt that's been planted. I'm probably thinking about this too much. Perhaps a good night's sleep will ease my mind off all of this."

I was hoping for a peaceful rest of the evening as I unwound, but as per usual in my life, a familiar voice would make her presence known so I could talk things out with her.

"I bet this wasn't an angle you thought could present itself," Karen commented.

"I sure as hell didn't think anything like that could possibly happen. I mean, I know in the early stages of any investigation, we have to look at all the scenarios. However, just the notion of him being a suspect based purely on location, timing, and circumstance. It just blows my mind."

"That's understandable. Outside of the Division, Phil is probably the best human friend you have. To hear that someone of such stature may be responsible for the deaths of two people is something that would be a shock to anyone's system."

"Believe me, it is. Granted, I know that this is just the first of a possibly long list of suspects we'll have as this case progresses, but for Jessica to immediately leap to him to start. I can't even begin to fathom why she would."

"I guess she thought given certain parameters in the preliminary findings, he might have fit the profile of the prime suspect. Sure, it is most likely premature to have fingered him right off the bat, but you have to keep in mind Jessica hasn't known Phil for as long as you have. She doesn't know all of his tendencies."

"That's true, I've known him for three years now; whereas Jessica only has for the past three months. That's a 12-to-1 ratio. So, I have a distinct advantage in that regard."

"Indeed, you do. So, while there is a probability that he wasn't responsible, you can't help but wonder if your opinion on the case isn't somewhat jaded because of how you value his friendship."

"Are you suggesting he may actually be guilty?" I accused.

"I'm not suggesting that at all. All I'm saying is that it's too early to know for certain. Until we get an estimated time of death on Dawkins and Simmons, and cross-reference that to the sign-in sheets at the rehab facility, you can't completely discount him entirely."

As much as I hated to admit it, my former fiancée was right. I couldn't rule my friend out; however, she did give me some clarity into the matter. Once I receive the findings from Forensics, I could check them against the records from the rehab centre, and be able to clear Phil's name; at least, for the time being. It was a notion that helped soothe my troubled psyche.

"Karen, you're a genius!" I replied. "As soon as Hutchins files her findings on the double homicide, I could get a warrant to search the attendance records for the group therapy sessions, and get my buddy off the hook. If you weren't a ghostly spirit, I would kiss you right now."

The spectre laughed, "Well, you could try, but I'm not sure if you would appreciate leaping out of your recliner and land face first onto the floor."

For the first time in the evening, I cracked a smile, and even shared a laugh over such a comedic prospect. "Thank you for that," I grinned. "I needed a mood changer."

"Anything to help, sweetie. Now, since you're in better spirits, are you going to turn in, or are you going to take some time to work on your novel writing project?"

I checked the time and debated about the options provided to me. "It's still a little early. I think I can boost my word count a bit before turning in."

Karen patted my shoulder. "I'll leave you be, so you can get to work on that."

"Much appreciated, Karen. And, thanks again."

"Anytime, dear," the spectre said, as she vanished into the night air.

I walked over to my desktop, fired up my word processing program, plugged in the USB drive that housed my work-in-progress, and started to type away on the document. I can't remember how many words I ended up typing that evening, but at least I was able to work away with a cleaner conscience. However, little did I realize, this good feeling would not last throughout the upcoming weekend.

CHAPTER 5

The next morning I headed into work at the Division with a bit of an upbeat attitude. It was something that wasn't lost on my partner who wondered if I had completely lost my mind.

"Well now," Jessica observed, "you seem to be in better spirits this morning. Have you slipped some sort of anti-depressants into your coffee?"

"No, I haven't, but I can see why you might think that."

"So, you're not upset that we interviewed Bennett last night over the Dawkins and Simmons case?"

"I will admit that I was disheartened over it when I got home last night." I leaned in to whisper to her. "But, after discussing things with Karen, she helped shed some perspective into the matter, and I'm hoping that when Hutchins and the Forensics Department release their findings, I could take the steps that will exonerate our friend."

"I hope you're right. I know how close the two of you are, but you have to realize where I was coming from."

"I do, and I don't fault you for doing so. We're trying to do our jobs and we have to explore every avenue out there while we hone in on the person, or people, responsible for this. There will be some cases over the course of our careers where family or friends might be initially believed to have been involved, and it will be hard then, too. We know within our hearts and minds that they're innocent, but until we get the concrete proof to state otherwise, we cannot rule anyone out."

Jessica breathed easier. "I'm glad you could see my side of things. So, now that we're on the same page, do you believe we should start canvassing the area to see if there were any eyewitnesses to the incident? Or, perhaps look at the security tape from the donut shop at Bedford and Bloor to see if we could find our shooter?"

"I believe we shall. I'll call to get a warrant, so we can get access to the security footage."

"No need," Jessica grabbed a fax off her desk. "I got it right here."

"Damn, you're quick. Let's get a move on then."

"I'm with you. With the Santa Claus Parade happening in a couple of days, I don't want any traces of a crime scene dampening the spirits of the children that will be lining the parade route."

"I hear you there." We began to make our way to the garage. "The last thing the young minds of today need is to be traumatized by something happening right in front of them and live. Today's choices for entertainment do that enough already."

~ * * * ~

After more banter about the ills of society today, the two of us proceeded to the aforementioned coffee shop where Dawkins and Simmons were last seen before they were slain. The coffee shop was busy, but that was understandable, given its location in relation to the university campus. However, there were a number of different coffee shop chains that dotted the 2.5 mile perimeter of the grounds. I figured the victims chose this particular chain because the coffee was quite good, and more affordable compared to the more upscale chains. Granted, nothing could compare to the ambiance of my preferred coffee house over on the Danforth near Donlands, but that was just a matter of personal preference.

Jessica and I requested to speak to the store manager. After we flashed our badges and showed him the search warrant, he allowed us access to the security tape. We were lucky to have gotten there when we did because had we waited another 30 minutes, the footage we were looking for would have been taped over. I hated the new systems that ran on a continuous tape loop where any archived footage got taped over with new material after 12 hours, but such is the way nowadays to make these systems more cost-effective to businesses.

My partner and I continued to analyze the footage, noticing the time Dawkins and Simmons left the store: 7:55 p.m. My heart sank with the knowledge Phil's group session meetings usually ended anywhere between 7 and 7:30; thus, allowing him a reasonable amount of time to have made his way from the rehab centre at College and Spadina to the area where the slayings took place. The dread I thought I had pushed aside was starting to creep back into my psyche when something came up to shoo it away again.

"Celdom," Jessica called to me. "Take a look at this."

I peered at the monitor and noticed a burly man with a thick winter jacket, designed with the black and blue colours and logos of an American football franchise attempting to further conceal an item within his cloak. I only caught a brief glimpse of the item, so my curiosity was piqued.

"Is there any way we can magnify this footage?" I questioned the manager.

A few button presses later and he was able to zoom in on the man in question. The magnification made the pixels a little grainy, but I could see the item shimmer in the store's outdoor lighting.

"This looks like our suspect with the possible murder weapon," I remarked.

Jessica agreed, "That's my belief, too." She turned to the store manager, and explained that we would have to seize the hard drive as evidence. The proprietor understood our plight, and handed over the storage device. We thanked him for his assistance and apologized again for the inconvenience this had caused.

~ * * * ~

As we walked back to our vehicle with the evidence in hand, I began to breathe easier.

"Well, that's a weight off of my shoulders," I commented. "When I saw the time on the surveillance footage, I was starting to worry that your earlier presumption might have been correct."

"You mean about Bennett being somehow involved in the murders?"

"Yes. However, considering he was wearing a different coloured winter jacket than the guy on the security tape, this clears his name."

Jessica was quick to correct me. "For the time being, at least. The tape only exposes one aspect of the incident. Until we get the reports back from Forensics, we can't rule him out entirely just yet."

I tried to grasp what my partner was saying. "Wait, are you insinuating that Bennett was wearing another winter jacket, killed Dawkins and Simmons, then changed into another coat by the time we met up with him at his place?"

"I'm not saying it's improbable, but it's not impossible either. After all, doesn't he always carry that black and grey knapsack with him? He could have been wearing the American football jacket over his regular coat and backpack, and then after the shooting disposed of the garment."

We got back to our car and stepped in. "You're not giving up on him being a possible suspect, are you?"

"Not for the time being, but hopefully, when we get this security cam footage back to the Division for further analysis, we'll have a more definitive answer."

I began to resent my girlfriend over the accusations. I knew she was trying to do a thorough job on this case, and I commended her for that. It was helping me get my shit together in the long run, as well. However, I still could not comprehend why she was so hung up on fingering Bennett all the while. Maybe I was being jaded by the friendship I shared with him over the past few years. From the novel writing group mass murders to the recent hostage situation, the two of us had been through a reasonable amount of stressful circumstances together. I felt he and I formed a kindred bond where the two of us could relate to one another. Now, because of the double homicide the night before, there was an insinuation that the guy I've grown to know and respect might not be who he portrayed himself as. I wanted to give him the benefit of the doubt, but if what Jessica was saying was true, and Bennett was a gun-toting killer? I didn't think I would be able to live with myself. Regardless of Jessica's pointed finger, I still clung to my beliefs that my best male friend was innocent of these alleged charges.

CHAPTER 6

Once Jessica and I arrived back at the Division, we beat a path to the Forensics Department. Tamara was at her desk and recognized the two of us approaching.

"Greetings, Detectives," she welcomed. "What's the latest from the streets?"

"We were able to get a hold of the security camera footage from the coffee shop where Dawkins and Simmons were last seen before they were shot," I informed.

"We think we have an image of the shooter," my partner added. "Is there any way yourself or anyone in your Department could enhance the footage, so we could get a clearer image of who we're after?"

"I'll get someone on it right away." Tamara got on her phone to call another member of the Forensics team in. Within a few minutes a young male came into his colleague's lab.

"You wanted to see me, Hutchins?" he enquired.

"Yes, I did." Tamara introduced. "Detectives Celdom and Amerson, this is Scott Harris. He's the member of the Forensics Department who usually handles video enhancement."

"Pleased to meet you, Detectives." Scott extended his hand.

Jessica shook the analyst's hands, followed by him shaking mine. "The pleasure is all ours, Harris," she said.

Scott Harris was indeed a young bloke; probably fresh out of university. He stood about 5'8" with a medium build, and sported brown hair that didn't extend halfway down his neck. Scott was reserved, but I could sense he was eager to help the two of us out.

"Hutchins said you had some security camera footage you needed to be spruced up?" he asked.

I produced the evidence. "We have the hard drive right here. We believe the person responsible for last night's double homicide by Varsity is on it."

"Well, let me take a look at it and see what I can do."

"That would be greatly appreciated," Jessica said.

~ * * * ~

The three of us proceeded over to the video lab to analyze the saved footage on the seized hard drive. The technician fast forwarded to the time frame we were interested in evaluating.

"Alright," Jessica recapped, while re-watching the images, "there's Dawkins and Simmons leaving together. Now, if we continue to let it roll, there should be a burly person wearing a blue and black winter jacket, trying to conceal something."

"Presumably, the murder weapon," I added.

"Let me slowly fast forward this footage to get to him." Harris slowed the footage down to a frame-by-frame slideshow.

A few seconds later, the man we were looking for appeared on the screen.

"Pause it right there," I requested.

"Is there any way we can enhance the video to make it less grainy?" Jessica posed.

"I can try my best, Detective Amerson." Scott went to work at his computer. He used the latest image editing software to bring some clarity to the images on the monitors.

"How does that look?" he asked.

"Works for me," my partner commented. "What about you, Celdom?"

I peered onto the screen and surveyed the pictures before me. Like I saw earlier, I could see the glint of the murder weapon inside of the puffy jacket; however, I was trying to see what the suspect wore underneath the black and blue-coloured winter wear.

"Can we zoom in on the jacket opening?" I asked.

"Sure thing, Detective Celdom." Scott complied by magnifying the image.

My heart sank a bit when I noticed what appeared like a swath of Hunter green within the opening of the jacket. The same shade of the coat Bennett wore when we met up with him at the coffee shop the previous evening. I could not believe it. I didn't want to believe it, but here was the proof staring right at me.

"What about the suspect's face?" I attempted to deflect the shocked expression I was letting seep through. "Can we make out any distinguishing features?"

"The face is pretty concealed," Scott replied. "I don't think I could enhance it any more than it already is."

"Are you sure?" I was getting frantic.

"Celdom, let it go." Jessica attempted to calm me down. "He's obviously a prime suspect now."

"No!" I shouted. "It's purely coincidental. He did not do it! I need some air."

I stormed out of the lab; knocking over some printouts in the process of my huff. Scott looked at Jessica confused, and wondered if I had gone off my nut. She didn't explain all the details to him, but defined it as a situation where the case had gotten personal to me. My partner didn't come after me right away, but did ask the analyst for copies of the suspect's images for the case files. Once Scott printed them off and handed them over, Jessica thanked him for his assistance, and apologized again for my outburst.

~ * * * ~

By the time my partner had located me, I was pacing in the Break Room; still fuming over the revelation. I was waiting for the coffee machine to finish producing the lousy swill it was renowned for when I slammed my fist into the front of the apparatus.

"Are you okay there?" Jessica questioned with caution.

"Am I okay? *Am I okay?* Do I fucking look okay to you, Amerson?!?"

"Celdom please, calm down?"

"Oh sure, calm down. Easy for you to say; you're not the one who's feeling how I am right now. Let me ask you something, Amerson, how would *you* feel if one of your best friends was being accused of killing two people, and the evidence was pointing a finger towards him? How would you react to such news, huh? I'd say about as torn as I fucking feel right now!"

I grabbed what was left of my coffee from the machine and rested my head against the automated device; letting out of frustrated sigh in the process.

Jessica chose her words carefully, "Celdom, I don't blame you for being upset. Hell, if I was in the same position you're in, I'd probably be experiencing the same emotions. Look, I don't know for certain if Bennett is really the guy we're looking for."

"Then why, Amerson?" I turned to face her, and leaned against the coffee machine with a hurt look in my eyes. "Why would my partner and girlfriend be so quick to suggest that my best friend is responsible for all of this?"

"I just noticed some possible motivators that may have given him a reason for such a crime."

"'Possible motivators? What? So he switched his allegiance to a rival club. So what if he's been battling mental health and addiction issues for years. While it's not the exact same classification, if I didn't know any better, I'd say it almost sounds a bit like a form of racial profiling."

Jessica slapped me across the face. "Damn it, Celdom, snap out of it! Besides, you should know by now that I don't engage in such tactics."

I began to simmer down, and sighed with resentment, "I'm sorry, Amerson. I just don't want to believe he's the guilty party here."

"Gary, sweetie, you're upset, frustrated, and confused. I can understand that given the circumstances. But, I'm worried about your actual stability given your reaction. Maybe you should book an appointment with Knoblach, so she could offer you some insight into why you believe what you think is true. Such a shock to the system would affect anyone."

I hung my head, drained, and emotionally exhausted. However, Jessica did offer a valid suggestion that could give me some assistance in getting to the root of my inner conflict. Perhaps the Police therapist could straighten me out, and help me get a better handle on the situation at hand.

"Maybe you're right, Amerson," I conceded. "Maybe I should talk to Knoblach about this. I am pretty shaken up over these possible findings."

"It couldn't hurt. Hopefully, she can help make sense of why you feel so conflicted. I just don't want you to go ape shit on anyone because of this case."

I took a deep breath. "You're right, I don't want to take this out on you, Benny, or anyone else. I'll call Knoblach and see if she could squeeze me in tomorrow."

"Thank you. This is a serious case, Celdom, and I want my partner's head fully in the game."

I thanked Jessica, and headed over to my desk. I knew my partner could be a real hard ass and stickler for details, but she – along with Karen – are good voices of reason. I'm thankful they were both in my life. I picked up my phone, and requested an appointment to see my therapist. It was the medicine I greatly needed at this point.

CHAPTER 7

The next day, I found myself in the office of the Police psychiatrist, Ann Knoblach. I had been going to see her for the past three years ever since my former girlfriend, Elaine Abraham, broke up with me after a very long and exhausting case. Looking back, I found it ironic that it was the same case where I would befriend the man who was a probable suspect in the murders of Brad Dawkins and Paula Simmons. It was a notion that ate away at me. I wanted to still hang onto the belief he was someone who was a victim of the "wrong area, wrong time" circumstance; however, the latest bit of evidence threw my illusion into complete disarray.

"So, Gary," Ann started, "you seemed really insistent on wanting to meet with me today. What seems to be troubling you? Is the spirit of your former fiancée becoming a conflict between yourself and your off-duty relationship with your partner?"

"No, it's not that at all. Karen and Detective Amerson have quite harmonious relations with one another; almost as if they were so-called 'gal pals." But, there's something that's messing with my mind and rationale regarding the latest case I've been working on."

The therapist looked puzzled. "The St. Lawrence Market robberies? You're not having any weird dreams relating to Detective Amerson involving various sausages, are you?"

I almost choked, "What? Oh hell, no; not anything resembling that! Besides, that case has been put to rest. I'm talking about the double homicide at the university a couple of night ago."

"You mean the Dawkins and Simmons murders, right?" Dr. Knoblach scribbled onto her notepad.

"Yes, that would be the investigation I'm talking about."

"Alright, so what exactly is bothering you about it?"

I took a deep breath and started to explain, "Well, there's something I saw while reviewing the surveillance tape from the coffee shop where Dawkins and Simmons were last seen alive. I got a look at the suspect caught on the tape, readying his weapon before heading after them, and my partner seems to believe that it is someone I know personally."

The therapist quirked her eyebrow. "Someone you know personally? You mean like a friend?"

"Yes, a close friend, if you could call it such. He's someone who I've come across on a couple of previous cases, but as an ally who happened to end up in the same situations I was in."

Dr. Knoblach scribbled in her notes. "An ally. This wouldn't happen to be that writer friend you met during the novel writing case three years ago, and ran into again during the hostage situation this past August, would it?"

"The very same. Amerson seems to think that since he was known to be at a location not even half a mile away around the time of the murders that he is a suspect."

"I see, and what has given your partner grounds to make such a presumption?"

"The two victims happened to be fans of the Canadian professional football club here in Toronto."

"The Boatmen, you mean?"

"Affirmative. Both Dawkins and Simmons were sporting vintage logo lapel pins of the franchise; although, when we interviewed my friend later that night, he explained that it might have been pins for the team's fan club."

"And, this was something he would recognize?"

"Bennett stated that he was a member of said fan club in the past; about 17 years ago. He mentioned the slight differences between the two logos."

"And your partner believed Bennett would have objected to their fandom?"

"In her eyes, she seems to think so. Due to some personal beliefs on his part, Bennett switched his fan allegiances over to the Boatmen's rival down in Hamilton."

Ann paused for a second. "Wait a minute, where does this Bennett live again?"

"Markham Road and Eglinton; out in Scarborough."

"So, I'm guessing he attends the games in Hamilton sporadically?"

"More than that. He's been a season ticket holder for the Ti-Cats for the past four years."

The therapist blinked. "You mean to tell me he makes the commute, some fifty miles away, multiple times of the year, just to watch football games?"

"It does seem farfetched when you first hear about it. However, there are fans of other teams who are as devoted as Bennett, if not more so."

"How so?"

"According to my friend, there is one particular devout group of fans out in Saskatchewan who will travel from all parts of the province down to Regina on a regular basis for the sheer purpose of cheering their favourite team. What's more, when the aforementioned Prairie club travels to different cities across the country to play, there will be pockets of fans turning up at those games; sporting their familiar green and white colours. He says they are a very hardcore fan base."

"That's not surprising. The same is true for our much maligned pro hockey club."

Dr. Knoblach and I broke into a debate about how popular our hockey team was in the city; trumping the fan bases for other teams within the city.

There wasn't a sporting event in Toronto where at least one attendee would show up wearing a jersey or T-shirt touting the hockey club. I commented that it was sickening to see a hockey team jersey at a baseball game, but the therapist used it as another example of how loyal fans could be to a particular franchise. But, that it was also a sign of civic pride. Even if it was for a franchise who hadn't won a championship in 45 years.

Dr. Knoblach asked, "So, getting back to your conflicted feelings about your friend, as it relates to this case; Detective Amerson's only belief that he is a suspect is because of this rival team fandom?"

I took a deep breath. "There's more to that. The reason why he was in the area was because he was at the rehab facility on Russell Street."

"Rehab facility? You mean he has an addiction issue?"

I nodded, "He does; he's a problem gambler. He's been seeking therapy for a few months now. In fact, Detective Amerson and I picked him up outside of the horse racing tele-theatre down where the old Greenwood racetrack used to be about a month and a half ago."

The therapist jotted down some more notes. "Really? And, how did you feel when you had to intervene in the situation?"

"It was difficult. He told my partner and me that he's had a gambling problem for years; stemming from his youth. He believes that his gambling issues are deeply engrained in his family's culture."

Dr. Knoblach looked confused. "His family's culture? I don't believe I follow."

"Bennett seems to think that his problems were inherited in grade school when his guardian included him in their hockey pool at work. He was only in it for 50 cents at the time, but half a dollar to a kid is quite a bit of money; especially back in the 70s. From there it expanded to gambling at school; setting up a pool for the American football championship game when he was in the Eighth Grade. He fell out of it for a while, since he was still underage, but once he became legal, it was when the million dollar weekly lotteries were all the rage, and he dived right into that. He seemed alright for the most part because he still had the even keel, but one night back in 2000 changed that."

"What happened then?"

"It was just after the racetrack slots opened up out by the airport."

"The one at Rexdale and 27?"

"The same. Bennett was originally going to go to a Boatmen game, but the matchup didn't quite appeal to him, so for a change of pace, he decided to head up there to try his hand at the one-armed bandits. So, according to him, he went in and sat down at one particular bank of quarter-slots, and he's playing, his balance is up and down, and then when he gets near the end of his credits, he hits a decent winning combination. It's nothing huge, but its mid-three figure range. And it was because of that he ended up getting hooked."

"That's not a good event to have happened to him. Some studies have shown that an early win could instill an addictive behaviour where you're constantly returning to the casino – or in this case, racetrack slot facility – in an attempt to recreate that momentary bit of luck."

"Exactly. In the years after that, he would make the odd trip up there; trying to match the success of that one night, and once in a blue moon, luck would find him again. But, more often than not, he would return to his home on the losing side of the ledger. What's more, he didn't limit his gambling activities to just by the airport. He's gone to Orillia, Niagara Falls, Brantford, Montréal, and Ottawa. Hell, he even admits sometimes when he goes down to visit his relatives for Christmas up in the Kawarthas; he would do a side trip to the racetrack slots there for a couple of hours. He was in pretty bad shape."

Dr. Knoblach agreed. "So, what happened that made your friend realize that he needed help?"

I took another deep breath. "According to Bennett, it was almost a year ago to the day. He had just finished the annual novel writing challenge -- a 50,000-word novel penned in 30 days – and he wanted to celebrate the accomplishment. So, he headed out to the racetrack slot facility out in Ajax."

"They have a facility out there? Isn't that only a quarter horse track?"

"It is, but they've had slots there for a few years now. In fact, a few months before they expanded the facility to add more machines. Anyway, Bennett went in with a set limit, and told himself once that was gone he was going to go home. Unfortunately, when you're an addict, you don't always listen to the voices of reason."

"He ended up gambling more than he intended?"

"All of the money he had earmarked for his Christmas shopping."

The therapist cringed. "Ouch!" That must have really depressed him."

"It did, but it really didn't hit home for him until he turned his cell phone on during the proverbial 'walk of shame' to check his messages, and noticed a text message from his girlfriend at the time; enquiring where he was. It was then he decided to come clean, and confess he had a problem."

"I'm going to guess she was not too impressed with him."

"She wasn't, which made him feel even worse. Here was Bennett, broke, dejected for gambling the money to buy Christmas presents for his family and friends, and now having to explain this to the first woman he'd been in a relationship with in a decade. Bennett was for certain she was going to break up with him on the spot. However, in a shocking turn of events, she gave him a proverbial 'stay of execution.'"

"She didn't dump him?"

"I have to admit, I was surprised when Bennett told me she supported him when he said he needed help. But, she did caution that if he did any major slip ups again, then he would end up alone. Bennett had some small blips along the way, but nothing as major as the Ajax incident. He even took a big step in his recovery by signing up for self-exclusion from all major gambling facilities in the province."

"So, that's why you picked him up outside of Greenwood back in September."

"Exactly. While self-ban doesn't apply to government-operated horse racing tele-theatres, like the one at Greenwood, Bennett was getting rather belligerent when he started to lose his shirt. He was escorted out of the facility, but surprisingly only given a warning. Had he been at the facility out by the airport and did that, he would've been charged with trespassing on the spot, and levied a hefty fine. Bennett was lucky the security at Greenwood were so lenient."

"However, as the arresting officers on the scene, didn't you or Detective Amerson handle his booking?"

Oh dear, apparently my typical lapse of judgment decided to make another appearance. It would have been proper protocol to have taken Phil in for questioning, and possibly give him time in a cell for him to cool off. If anything, Jessica and I should have had a long discussion with him over the circumstances; that much we did do. Not just because we were the first officers on the scene, but his friends, as well.

"There were no official charges filed by the security at the facility since this was Bennett's first infraction," I recollected. "Detective Amerson and I did lecture him about what would happen should he have found himself at that location again and caused another scene; a warning he understood and complied with."

"So, he's been staying clean from gambling for the most part since then?"

"To the best of my knowledge, he has. He has admitted to a few lottery purchases once in a blue moon, but those are becoming fewer than they had been before he started seeking help for his addiction. The incident at Greenwood was the only serious event he's had."

"And, you said your friend has been seeking treatment now for almost a year, correct?"

"He sought help into his gambling problem shortly after the Ajax incident last November 30th, yes." Bennett has stated that he's been going to one-on-one sessions with his addictions counsellor at a location within Scarborough since December, but it's only been since February he's been going to group sessions down on Russell Street."

"So, let me recap what you've told me so far: You've been working on this double homicide since last night, and your partner seems to believe that your friend – who has a sporting rivalry with an opposing team that the two victims support, and was a half a mile away attending an appointment around the time of the murders – is a suspect in the slayings."

"That is correct, Dr. Knoblach."

"So, when Detective Amerson came to you with these suspicions, how did it make you feel?"

"Admittedly, I was shocked at the accusations. I mean, outside of the Division, Bennett is probably my best friend. I was so certain he could not have been the one to have committed such a heinous crime. I know he's not perfect with his addiction issues, but I don't think his gambling would ever push him to the point where he would actually go out and kill anyone. If anything, because of his problem, it might lead him into a downward spiral of depression that might end up in him committing suicide; heaven forbid."

"But, the mind of someone who suffers from an addiction of any sort could cause a distortion of one's thinking patterns. In the case of some individuals, they may feel so angry and upset over a huge loss, they will end up blaming others for their predicament."

I blinked at my therapist. "Are you saying that Bennett might have been one of these people who got so emotionally agitated over a recent loss, he would take out that aggression on someone else in a delusional bid for revenge?"

"That could occur in some of the more extreme cases, but if assault and battery is possible – combined with a robbery attempt – homicide could also result should the individual not be in the right frame of mind."

"But, there wasn't a robbery attempt. The Forensics team that was at the crime scene stated that neither Dawkins' nor Simmons' possessions were disturbed. It was almost as if they were targeted for a specific reason; however, the only possible motive we've been able to come up with is they happened to be fans of the local Canadian professional football club."

"So, it could have possibly been your friend -- or a different fan from their rivals -- who could have fired the fatal shots."

"It may appear that way. However, Bennett pointed out that the Boatmen have more than one rival. Sure, there are Ti-Cat supporters from down Hamilton way, but he did make note of the American football club from down in Buffalo who have sporadically played games here over the past few years. He seems to believe that it might have been one of their supporters who would prefer the American game to usurp the gridiron landscape here in Toronto."

Dr. Knoblach leaned forward. "And, is that something you believe to be possible?"

"Honestly, don't know what to believe. Bennett could be right, Amerson could be right; hell, it might be something else entirely. All I know is I'm feeling like I'm caught in the middle between what my partner wants to believe, and what I want to believe. I'm completely torn on the matter, Dr. Knoblach."

The therapist sighed. "Celdom, I don't know what I could do to help you. You're feeling conflicted right now about this case, but it's too early in the investigation to know exactly what will actually transpire. The only advice I can give you right now is to continue working on it until the situation clears up. That being said, when it does, and you still feel yourself in this quandary, please don't hesitate to book another appointment, so we can discuss this further, alright?"

Well, there's a dead end that I wasn't expecting. Here I was, trying to get some clarity on what was troubling me, and the only thing Knoblach had for me was to "stay the course" until the waters became less muddy. All I had been able to do was vent and not get any real answers. While I thanked the therapist for her time, I left her office in a bit of a foul mood. I didn't even get the opportunity to explain the evidence from the hard drive which Jessica believed further implicated Phil in the murders. I was ready to tear a strip off the next person who came up to me. However, when I saw that happened to be Lt. Davies, I decided it was better to hold my tongue.

"Where the hell have you been, Celdom?" he demanded.

"A thousand pardons, Lieutenant. I was in an appointment with Dr. Knoblach. What's the situation, sir?"

My commanding officer's voice grew solemn. "I want you and Amerson to head on over to the movie theatre at Richmond and John. There's been a triple homicide."

I kept my composure for the time being, but in the back of my mind, I wondered if it was the same person responsible for the Dawkins and Simmons murders, but also hoped that my previously accused friend didn't leave anything to implicate himself in these, as well.

CHAPTER 8

Jessica and I bolted to the movie theatre at the corner of Richmond and John as soon as Lt. Davies informed us of the latest slew of killings. I had worried this would be a carbon copy of the brutal murders that occurred earlier in the year when some nut bar in Colorado opened fire on a crowded cinema during an opening day screening of the latest offering from a superhero franchise. By the time the violence had ended in the Denver suburb, there were 12 people dead – including the shooter – and 59 others wounded. I was praying the carnage at the theatre here wasn't as catastrophic, but both my partner and I had to see to be certain.

Once we arrived, there were a couple of ambulances still outside the facility, and the entrance was lined with yellow police tape. It was a brutal scene, but not as bad as I had initially feared. Jessica and I flashed our badges, and made our way to the heart of the crime scene: one of the screening rooms on the upper level of the building. The two of us were met once again by Forensics Investigator, Tamara Hutchins.

"Miss Hutchins," I greeted. "We meet again."

"Unfortunately," my partner added, "not in the friendliest of circumstances. What is the situation here?"

"By the looks of things, a smaller version of the Colorado cinema shooting from earlier this year. Three people are dead, and nine others wounded by the end of the carnage."

"Any possible motive in this assault?" I queried.

"Undetermined at the present juncture. However, based on what was in your initial findings from the Dawkins and Simmons murders a couple of days ago, I believe they are possibly related."

"How do you figure?" I asked.

"You didn't notice the movie poster on your way in?"

"Not really."

"They are in the midst of a football-themed film festival at this theatre to coincide with the Canadian Football Championship taking place in town next week."

"Football-themed film festival," Jessica began to clue in. "Of course, it all makes sense now. The Boatmen pins on Dawkins' and Simmons' jackets, and now the mass shootings during the film festival. Whoever is responsible for this is a serial killer designed to make the upcoming Championship's festivities a statement."

"It appears that way," I remarked, "but, against what?" I thought about it for a moment; then, it dawned on me. "Wait a minute, nine people injured? Are you thinking what I'm thinking, Amerson?"

"Find out where one of the wounded is being treated, and question them for more details?"

"You read my mind." I turned my attention to Tamara. "Hutchins, could you forward a report on this triple homicide to either Detective Amerson or me, so we can add it to the existing case file?"

"That's what I'm paid to do, isn't it?"

"Thank you kindly." I said before making my way back downstairs.

"This is greatly appreciated, Hutchins," Jessica added.

"Just glad to help, Detectives." Tamara resumed her task at hand.

~ * * * ~

As my partner and I walked down the stairs back to street level, we were joined by a familiar presence.

"So, you two finally have your first lead on the case, eh?" Karen posed.

"At least, one that's not based on hunches," I commented with my tongue firmly planted in my cheek.

"Oh, let it go, Celdom," Jessica rolled her eyes. "It was purely a suspicion."

"And so far, an unfounded one."

"At least it was something we had a lead on. All you've been doing since I brought his name up is attempting to disprove that he is a possible suspect."

"And, all you've had so far is circumstantial belief. The insinuation that he was in the area for different matters, and the fact he is a rival supporter is purely speculative. There is no concrete proof that confirms he's the guy behind all of this."

"'No concrete proof'? Celdom, I know you're getting up there in years, and your memory may not be as good as it used to be, but are you telling me that you're discounting the security cam footage Harris analyzed for us yesterday?"

"She does have a point, Gary," Karen chimed in. "It may not be the clearest of evidence, but it does provide some reasonable proof that it might be your friend."

"Oh, so now you believe her too?" I snapped at the spectre. "All you two have is an image of a bulky jacket with what looks like a swath of Hunter green inside of it. It could be purely coincidental, but I still attest that it is not Bennett."

"Then prove to us that it's not him," Jessica challenged. "Call him on his cell phone, and see what he has to say about the latest."

"Do you doubt my resolve?"

"We're just saying, give him a chance to show us he's the innocent guy you say he is," Karen offered. "Unless, you are not sure that he is."

"Alright," I pulled out my phone. "I'll call him right now to get you two to drop this."

I dialed Phil's number and waited for a response; all the while, I was showing a confident bravado that the girls thought was a facade. However, my demeanor changed slightly when an automated voice on the other end of the line informed me that my call could not be completed at that time. A smirk began to form on Jessica's face.

"What's the matter, Celdom?" she mocked. "Is our prime suspect not picking up?"

"Screw off, Amerson. It's saying that he can't be reached. He's probably somewhere where there is no signal."

"Like riding the subway home from the scene of today's triple homicide."

"Don't be too sure of that, Jessica," Karen corrected. "Didn't Bennett say he was participating in a writing session of the subway this weekend?"

"He did," Jessica said, "but, those events are usually held on a Sunday; today is Saturday."

"They changed it up this year," I informed. "Since tomorrow is the Santa Claus Parade downtown, they switched it to today, so they could avoid the crowds heading down for the event."

"So, that's probably it," Karen concluded. "His phone doesn't get a signal underground; ergo, he can't be reached. You should try again later when he's back home, or on the bus back from Kennedy Station. Then, you should be able to get the answers you're looking for."

Jessica resigned for the time being. "Okay, we'll try again later, but I'm not dropping it just yet."

"And speaking of answers," Karen continued, "shouldn't you two be heading to the hospital to interview one of the shooting victims?"

"She does have a point," I agreed. "We should get a move on. Sunnybrook is a fair drive from here."

My partner sighed over the fact her hunch had to be put on the backburner for now, but realized she still had a job to do. The two of us piled into our vehicle, and commenced our trip to one of the main health care facilities in the city. Jessica still held onto the belief that in some shape or form, Phil was implicated in this whole mess. I believed that one of the victims would dispel her intuition, but in the instance of some people, they can be very set in their ways. It was one of the things that can be a boon and a curse in any relationship. I just didn't know what side of the coin would turn up.

CHAPTER 9

As much as it was a morbid way to think, I was glad the shootings at the movie theatre happened on a Saturday. It meant for a less congested drive along the Don Valley Parkway up to Sunnybrook. Granted, we also had the option of taking the Bayview extension up to the health care facility, but I thought the midtown expressway would be easier and quicker. It certainly makes for a scenic drive; unfortunately, the fall colours had already come and gone by this time of year, so I was left to see a collection of bare branches and plain evergreens that lacked a wintery coat of white. The temperatures were cool, but not cold enough to bring the first snows of the season to the bulk of the city. I hoped that would change over the upcoming weeks as the festive season drew near. I was always one for a white Christmas.

I snapped back to my senses when I saw the turnoff for Eglinton Avenue. The rest of our drive would take us through the northern part of the Leaside neighbourhood before we arrived at the grounds of Sunnybrook. It is by far, the largest health care facility in all of Toronto; complete with its own residence for war veterans. It saddened me a bit that most of those who had fought in the two World Wars had passed on, but I was always grateful for the service they gave our country in those conflicts. It's the courage and bravery they exuded that is lost on today's generation. Sure, you had the recent mission in Afghanistan, and to some that is the war they are most familiar with. However, to me, the war vets of yore are indeed 'the forgotten generation', and I don't intend to forget them.

Upon arriving at the Reception Desk in emergency, Jessica and I showed our badges, and enquired where we could find one of the victims from the shooting, a Wayne Lottridge – identified to us by one of the paramedics we spoke to over Jessica's phone while in transit. We were told to wait until he cleared Triage, but were cautioned that it would probably be a while until he was. My partner and I understood, so we headed elsewhere in the facility in a bid to find a decent cup of coffee. Much to our surprise, we found a kiosk from one of the more upscale coffee chains near the main entrance offering better than average swill. It was along the lines of the notable American style shops that would sell a fancy-assed mug of mud for $6, but this was purely a Canadian-made retailer. To this day, I don't think I will ever understand the concept of all this 'low fat, half-cap, skinny latte' crap, but if that's what appeals to the consumer, then all the power to them. I was fortunate the chain offered basic flavoured coffees; something that admittedly interests my palate. I eventually settled for a medium-sized cup of Irish Cream, taken black with a couple packets of artificial sweetener; while Jessica opted for a small-sized serving of the medium-roast. She always was simplistic in her beverage choices.

After grabbing our drinks, we made our way back to the Emergency Ward, and prepared to wait for however long it would be before we were able to talk to Lottridge. In the meantime, my partner and I decided to engage in a little small talk.

"This must be a different experience for you. Being in the Emergency Wing at a hospital where you're *not* a patient?" I could tell Jessica's comment was dripping with sarcasm.

I played off the verbal jab, "Give it time, Amerson. I highly doubt this case will be over once we talk to the victim. If history is due to repeat itself, I'll be back at St. Mike's before you know it."

"I'm surprised about something. Most trauma cases in the city are usually transported here; yet, whenever you get banged up you're sent downtown. Why is that?"

"I guess there's some sort of special arrangement the Division has with the facility down there. Probably because of proximity and what not. However, since they have an excellent staff of doctors here, and the space at St. Mike's is rather limited, they shuttle them to Sunnybrook instead."

"You would think you'd be treated more often here because this is closer to your home."

"Actually, the nearest hospital to me is East General over at Coxwell and Mortimer; kitty-corner from the old East York Municipal Offices. But, they don't have the facilities or manpower to treat all of my injuries, so I end up at Queen and Victoria instead. It makes for a bitch when I'm eventually discharged – come to think of it, it's a pain regardless of whichever hospital I'm sent to because of where my home is – but, I've grown accustomed to it for the past 27 years. It's just part of adapting to life in the city."

"Have you ever thought of moving to a different part of Toronto? You've been living at your little bungalow around Pape and Cosburn for quite a while now, haven't you?"

"For my entire career, I have. I've thought about moving to a different area a few times. Hell, I even remember when Karen and I first met, she suggested I move out to Edmonton, and move in with her."

"Was that something you were exploring in the lead-up to your wedding?"

"I was considering it. I even had the application in to transfer out to the Alberta capital. I was just waiting to pull the trigger until after I came back from our honeymoon. Unfortunately, both you and I know what happened on what was supposed to be our wedding day, so after I came back from the funeral, I revoked my request, and here I am today; two decades later with you as both my work colleague, and the special woman in my life."

"I'm thankful you're in my life too, Celdom. But, I'm curious about something. If you were to ever move out of your current house – and stay within the city – where would you want to live?"

I had a feeling she was leading me onto something. Could Jessica have been giving some thought into the presumption Tamara made a couple days ago, and was considering the two of us live together under the same roof? I had to be careful with what I was going to say next because I didn't know how she would react. If it wasn't something she was thinking about, and I were to say the Cabbagetown area, that might upset her because I might come across as too eager. If I were to say I liked where I had been living for close to half of my life, I might get accused of being stuck in a rut, and not open to a possibility of change; which seems rather silly since I've dealt with change throughout my career: different partners, different superior officers. Even the addition of little Benny seven years ago could be argued as a change in my life. It would be a matter of trying to adapt.

I took a sip of my coffee. "To be honest," I said, "I really haven't given it much thought. While, I admit I'm okay with where I've been living for that past 25-some-odd years, there's part of me that is enticed by the thought of living elsewhere. I've contemplated about relocating closer to the Division so I wouldn't have a long commute to work – not that it's a huge trek to begin with – but, with perhaps another 5 years or so left in my career, would it even be worth it in the long run? But, we're only weighing in on one side of the debate, what about you? If you had the opportunity to move to anywhere in Toronto, where would it be, or would you prefer to stay in your Wellesley and Parliament-area townhouse?"

Jessica paused for a moment to contemplate my return query before offering her response. "I don't know. While I do like my little townhouse, sometimes I think it's too quaint. It's a decent size, so I have a fair amount of space within it. But, it seems too quiet at times. It's almost as if it feels a little empty to me."

"Maybe you should get yourself a pet of your own to give the abode a little more character."

"Like maybe a canine, for example?"

"It doesn't have to be a dog. It could be a bird, or a cat. Some animal that won't make you feel so alone when you're off-duty. But, just out of curiosity, if it did happen to be a four-legged friend with a wagging tail, what sort of breed would you be interested in?"

"Well, you might think it's kind of silly."

"Amerson, nothing is too silly when considering adding a pet to one's life; unless, it's an unreasonable addition to the individual's lifestyle."

"True enough," my partner agreed. She was about to tell me the breed she desired when the doctor came to inform us that Lottridge had just gotten out of Triage and was being located to a room up on the 4th floor of the hospital. Jessica and I thanked the physician for the information, and began to make our way to where he was recuperating. However, in the back of my mind, I was wondering what my girlfriend's answer would have been.

~ * * * ~

Upon arriving at the room, we found the shooting victim conscious, and being visited by a woman. My partner and I presumed it was a loved one, and were cautious of interrupting the duo. We gingerly knocked on the door, and entered the hospital room.

"Mr. Lottridge?" I began.

"Yes," he confirmed. "Can I help you?"

"Our apologies for the intrusion," I introduced, while we flashed our badges. "Toronto P.D., I'm Detective Celdom, and this is Detective Amerson."

"We wanted to ask you a few questions regarding the events that led to your stay here at Sunnybrook," Jessica added.

"Do you want me to leave?" the female visitor asked the man lying in bed.

"That's not necessary, Miss...?" I assured.

"Toni Lottridge, I'm Wayne's sister."

"His sister?" Jessica asked. "You were not with him in the theatre when the shooting occurred?"

"No, I was at work when I received the call that Wayne had been shot. I rushed up here from Mississauga as soon as I found out."

Based on Miss Lottridge's attire, it looked like she was employed in a fast food restaurant. Ironically, her uniform was similar to the chain of coffee shops Jessica and I interviewed Bennett in a few nights before. It shouldn't have come to any surprise to me, as their locations seem to be dotted all over the Greater Toronto Area.

"So, I'm presuming the two of you live in separate residences?" I questioned.

"Yes, Detective," Mr. Lottridge mentioned, "Toni lives in Mississauga with our parents, while I have my own apartment in The Annex."

"And how long have you been living on your own, Mr. Lottridge?"

"For six years now," he replied. "I was starting my own business downtown, and didn't want to have to commute back and forth to Peel Region, so I relocated to within the city."

"Excuse me for prying, but what type of business is it that you operate?"

"I run a consulting firm down in the St. Lawrence area."

"So, with it being the weekend, you had the day off, and decided to take in a movie down in the Entertainment District, correct?"

"That's correct. I had heard they were running football-themed movies at the theatre this week as part of the run-up to the Championship game next week, so I decided to take in one of the screenings. I just didn't expect to wind up in hospital because of it."

"Most movie goers usually don't," Jessica noted. "Could you please recount what happened in the theatre for us, Mr. Lottridge?"

"Certainly, Detective Amerson. I was watching the movie, minding my own business like everyone in the theatre was, when this madman stormed into the central aisle and started shooting everything in the auditorium."

"Did the shooter yell anything while he was firing?"

"It's funny, almost ironic. He didn't start until the famous line; 'Show me the money!' was uttered on the screen, then the shooter exclaimed, 'I've got your money right here!' and started spraying bullets. I tried to dive for cover, but ended up getting hit before I got to safety."

"You were very lucky, brother," Toni noted.

"Indeed, he was," I added. "Was that the only thing he was screaming during the onslaught?"

"Yes, he was babbling something about 'death to Canadian football,' and 'American football is the Master game.' It just seemed so deranged that he would do it during a movie screening, and not at any other event closer to the game."

My partner and I looked at each other and gave a silent nod in affirmation. "Now, Mr. Lottridge, I know you might not have had an opportunity to do so because it was dark within the auditorium, but were you able to get a good look at the shooter?"

"It was very dark, but thankfully, the light from the projector did highlight some of his features."

"So, the shooter was a male then," Jessica observed.

"Very much so. I could detect a little bass in his voice. He was a tall guy; probably just over 6-feet, and wearing a blue and black jacket, embroidered with an American football team's logo on the left breast."

"Did he have any other distinguishing characteristics?"

"He did look like he was sporting a moustache," Wayne noted. "Probably one of those 'Movember' participants; you know, the people who raise funds for prostate cancer research by growing facial hair for the month. Oh, and he had medium-length dark hair. Not quite down to his shoulders, but about midway down the back of his neck."

"Was he wearing any headwear," I asked, "a winter hat, a baseball cap, anything of the sort?"

"It did look like he was wearing a winter cap, red in colour, if I'm not mistaken. It didn't look like he was very colour co-ordinated with the rest of his ensemble."

Jessica and I continued to interview Mr. Lottridge about other details regarding the shooting for a little while longer. We informed him of the three lives lost in the carnage, a factoid that brought sorrow to him, but made him realize how fortunate he was to have been one of the relatively lucky ones. We concluded our questioning, and thanked him and his sister for their time, and wished him a speedy recovery.

~ * * * ~

As we walked back to our vehicle, we discussed the case in a little more detail.

"So, what do you think?" Jessica asked me. "Do we have enough information to query the database for possible suspects on file?"

"We can give it a shot, and see what turns up," I pondered. "But, hopefully this will exonerate Bennett from being a possible suspect."

"Look, Celdom. I know this whole debate of whether or not he did or didn't is straining our solidarity. You have your opinion, and I have mine, so let's just agree to disagree until there is more concrete proof that states otherwise. Besides, despite everything else, we still have a cold blooded killer still walking the streets who has killed five people. We both need to get him behind bars before he strikes again."

"You're right, Amerson. We're losing sight of our objective here, and that's to get this guy locked up. This constant bickering about whether or not a certain friend is a guilty party is distracting us from doing our job effectively. We both need to get back on the same page here. Hopefully, the database will turn something up."

The two of us climbed into our car and began the drive back to the Division. Jessica and I hoped there would be another break in this psychopath's carnage. Unfortunately for us, it wouldn't be too long before he struck again, and at a more visible event.

CHAPTER 10

The sun rose the next day, and there was a distinct nip in the air. It still wasn't cold enough for snowflakes to fall from the heavens, but it was still a day full of excitement for young children across the Greater Toronto Area. For today was the November day they all had anticipated for months. It was the day the annual Santa Claus Parade took over the streets of the city.

I awoke from my bed the same way I normally would on a Sunday while I was in the midst of an investigation: far too early, and in dire need of some coffee. The query Jessica and I did of our criminal database the night before turned out to be a dead end. Whoever was responsible for the recent string of homicides was a fresh face on Toronto's blood-soaked streets, and it would take a more concentrated effort to discover who he was and what his true motives were. However, what Mr. Lottridge stated in his interview at Sunnybrook did coincide with Bennett's suspicions; a possible pro-American football fan who wanted the Canadian version of the gridiron abolished forever, so it would help pave the way for the variation popular south of the 49th parallel to set up permanent shop here in the Great White North. It sounded like a ludicrous notion, however, with the fact that the Canadian football Championship Game was scheduled to be played one week from today, I figured this madman thought it would be the most opportune time to make his bold statement heard: when the eyes of the entire country were focused on 'The Big Smoke' for the Canadian sporting event of the season. Regardless, there were five innocent local sports fans that had lost their lives and another nine people injured, thanks to this wacko. We needed to get him off the streets, but we were having a difficult time finding out who he was in the first place.

I stumbled into the bathroom for my usual morning cleanse, and attempted to picture our suspect in question. All we had was his attire, and a few physical features, but nothing more substantial than that. Was he

Caucasian, African-Canadian, family man, part of a street gang, tied to an underground mob, or just some nut who wants to further Americanize the Canadian landscape? These were all little intricacies that I was mulling over in my mind, but I kept drawing a blank. After I dried myself off from my shower, I wiped the steam from the bathroom mirror, looked at my face, and resigned myself to the notion that for the lack of any further leads, I had to wait until he made his next move. It wasn't something I wanted to do, but it was the only recourse I had at the time.

Once I got dressed, I took Benny out for his morning constitutional, and also to clean up any 'fun presents' he left behind. During my walk, I was surprised to see my dog sitter, Geny Phillips, strolling along the streets with her golden doodle, Siren, in tow.

"Geny?" I called out to her. "Is that you?"

Geny greeted me with a hug. "Hello, Gary. How are you doing?"

"A little worn with the latest case that I'm working on, but that's nothing new. What are you doing up here in East York? Is your usual route in Leslieville getting too boring for Siren?"

"It's not that. I hadn't seen or heard from you in a while, so I figured I drop by for a visit to see how you were."

With the previous St. Lawrence Market robbery case ending just as the football homicide investigation was starting, I hadn't had a chance to meet up with Geny for a social visit. As part of my normal day off routine, I'd go down to her place, or we'd meet up in The Beach and take our dogs out for a walk along the boardwalk. Regardless of what we ended up doing, there was always a spot of tea had between us, along with some good conversation. I guess she thought I had gotten into trouble, or ended up in St. Mike's again, and was worried for my health and safety. Although, judging by how her golden doodle was snuggling up to my husky, it appeared that Siren was missing Benny's company as much as Geny did hanging out with me. I explained to my friend what had happened, and she understood my situation.

"Do you have any plans for today?" Geny asked.

"None as of yet, but that could change at the drop of a hat. What did you have in mind?"

"Well, I figured since I was in the neighbourhood, and it's been a while since we've seen each other, I was hoping we could walk the dogs around the neighbourhood, and then head to your place for a spot of tea. Maybe we could even watch the Santa Claus Parade on the telly while we catch up on things?"

"Considering the circumstances, I think that is a novel idea. I must warn you, my place is a bit of a mess, so you'll have to excuse its appearance."

"That's not a problem. This visit was unannounced, so I understand if your abode is not the most spic-and-span dwelling."

I chuckled over Geny's comment, but I always enjoyed spending time with her. I had known her ever since I've had Benny, when I needed someone to look after the little guy whenever I was away for a big case, or at a conference. Since then, the two of us became close friends to the point where one might argue that we were siblings; it was that significant of a bond. She was one of the few people I could talk to about my issues with Karen, and was a sounding board when the entire mess with Elaine occurred. Later, she became a supporter when I began my outside-of-work relationship with Jessica, and has heard me out as I rode the rollercoaster of emotions pertaining to dating my partner. It's funny, to an outsider they might have asked me after the Elaine fiasco, "Why don't you start dating Geny? You two get along so well together, and your pets really hit it off with each other." To that I responded with the fact that Geny and I don't see each other that way. Sure, the thought might have crossed my mind once, but I didn't want to jeopardize the good, close friendship the two of us shared with one another. Relationships come and go over the course of one's life, but a best friend – at least, in the male-female capacity – is hard to come by.

~ * * * ~

The four of us returned to my little bungalow after our walk and began to get settled. I checked my pantry for what tea I had on hand that I could offer my guest. After a bit of discussion with her, we settled on a vanilla-flavoured oolong, and I prepared some hors d'oeuvres to go along with it. We let the dogs play out in my backyard while the two of us sat on my back porch; keeping an eye on the canines.

"So," Geny began, "what's the deal with this latest case you're working on?"

"Well, here's the situation. As I was finishing up the final reports on this case Jessica and I had been working on regarding a bunch of robberies down at St. Lawrence Market this past Thursday, we get assigned a case regarding a couple of homicides up on the university campus by Queen's Park."

"Talk about a change of gears."

"So, we're doing the preliminary investigation, and figure it's just the double homicide, then yesterday, there's an added shooting down at the movie theatre in the Entertainment District; three dead, and nine others wounded. Both of the incidents are related."

"That's terrible. Has there been a description of the shooter yet?"

"The only thing we have to go on so far, is that he's a tall man, over 6-feet, medium-length hair and a moustache. Oh, and in both incidents, he was wearing a black and blue-coloured winter jacket; emblazoned with the logo of an American football team."

"That's not really much to go on."

Part of Mr. Lottridge's account came back to me. "Wait, it was reported by one of the wounded in the theatre shooting that he was uttering anti-Canadian football sentiments."

"So, these are possibly targeted shootings?"

"It would appear like they are. The murderer appears to be targeting fans of the Boatmen; you know the Canadian football team they have playing down at the domed stadium?"

"Isn't that where they're going to be playing that big Championship game next week?"

"It is. Actually, the University Championship game is being played there on the Friday night, and the Professional Championship on Sunday night."

"That is definite cause for concern. If what you're saying about the shooter is correct; then, he might be targeting not only Argo fans, but other fans who'll be attending those games."

I weighed what my friend said. "Well, it looks like he's targeting the events around them, so there is probably a good chance he might try to hit those events too."

Geny began to worry. "And, that is a scary notion unto itself."

I had to admit, I was becoming concerned myself. There were going to be fans from across the country – and some from the United States, as well – converging on the city over the next few days to not only take in the two contests on the field, but all of the festivities around the downtown core to celebrate the Championship. Whenever the end of November rolls around, whatever metropolis hosts the big game turns into one huge party with all of the events being held in the week beforehand. All of the teams throw get-togethers to honour not only their own fans, but others of rival clubs. There is not much of a "melting pot" mentality in Canada, but one could argue that when it's Canadian Football Championship Week, fans of all of the league's eight franchises – including fans of clubs that have come and gone – unite as one massive collective to get their drink on. I guess that's why some people call it the "Grand National Drunk."

This year's edition had the added significance because it was be the 100th time the Championship game was to be played. Over the years, there had been university clubs and professional franchises contesting for the prized chalice. During the Second World War, there were even military branches that had competed for the trophy. The common bond between most of these organizations was they were based within Canada; all except one particular franchise in the mid-90s. Between 1993 and 1995, the Canadian professional football body experimented with establishing teams with the United States of America. The first such club set up shop in Sacramento, California. In the final two years of the trial, Canadian football ended up being played in San Antonio, Las Vegas, Memphis, Birmingham, and Shreveport. However, the most successful of the American-based teams was one who set up shop in Baltimore. In both years they were in operation, Baltimore played well enough to advance to the Championship game; losing in Vancouver in 1994, but proving victorious a year later when the game was held in Regina, Saskatchewan. Many critics called it a sad day when the illustrious trophy was awarded to a club that called a city south of the 49th parallel home. However, there ended up being a shining light at the end.

Most of the American-based clubs fared poorly on the balance sheet, and ended up folding. Baltimore was the only successful team during the experiment, but was forced to relocate when a spiteful American football team's owner decided to move his embattled club from Cleveland to the Maryland metropolis near Chesapeake Bay. As a result, the homeless club moved north of the border to become the current incarnation of the franchise in Montréal; which had seen much success during the previous 16 seasons. Yet, even after the club left the U.S. before the start of the 1996 season, there were still fans in Baltimore who support the Canadian game, and a few even make the trip north of the border to attend the Championship Game party events. While the team in their newfound home had become the envy of most of the other teams based on their performance on the field, they certainly were not the most popular. That designation, as I recall Bennett telling me, was reserved for the fan base of Regina.

I wasn't sure if it was because it was a community-based franchise – complete with the opportunity via a fundraising drive to own 'shares' of the team – or the fact the entire Prairie province of Saskatchewan came out to cheer them on, but they are staunch supporters of the 101-year old club.

What's more, their fans are not just concentrated within the borders of the rectangular province, but throughout the entire country. Some may argue within the confines of professional hockey, "Who is Canada's Team?", and most people would say the long-running clubs in Montréal or Toronto; although, that tends to get altered once May and June rolls around to "whichever Canadian franchise gets furthest in the playoffs." However, when it comes to Canadian football, if you're basing purely on nationwide fan support, then it is the little club that plays on Piffles Taylor Way out in the capital city of the province of Saskatchewan.

At the time of my little meeting over tea and hors d'oeuvres with Geny, it was undetermined who would be playing at the professional Championship game the following week. That was to be decided later on in the day when the divisional finals were to be played. In one contest, the Boatmen had gone on the road to play the usually successful squad from Montréal. The later match featured the side from Calgary travelling to the Pacific Coast to compete against the defending champions out of Vancouver. If Vancouver and Montréal ended up winning their games, they would convene at the domed stadium downtown seven days from now in a rematch of last year's Championship. I didn't have any particular favourite team that I was cheering for. My main concern was to make sure there were no further incidents involving our little gun-toting maniac. I only hoped Jessica and I would be able to capture him before the Big Party was ruined even further. Geny noticed that I was a little tense with my mind racing over the psychopath, and suggested that I try to not think about it by watching the Santa Claus Parade; which was about to start its broadcast. I agreed that it was a great suggestion, so I walked over to my TV, turned it on, and tuned into this year's coverage.

I have to admit, I had always loved the Parade. It's an event people of all ages could enjoy; the marching bands playing Christmas music, the colourful floats full of magical wonder, and of course, the big guy wearing the red suit, riding the sleigh at the very end. It was something that brought out the kid in all of us, and a sure sign that winter was upon us. I still had to shake my head over the fact that Toronto's Santa Claus Parade was first started back in 1905. For the majority of its lifespan, it had been sponsored by one of the most famous of department store chains in Canadian history. Alas, the store's association of the event ended back in 1982, and was threatened to be cancelled. However, thanks to some generous corporations, the annual tradition was saved, and has continued to run ever since. Part of the corporate generosity was the institution of "corporate celebrities" dressed up as clowns who would march down the Parade route from Christie Pits down to the St. Lawrence Market area, and entertain all of the children along the way. While the route has changed over the years, one thing it has always done, for as far back as I can remember, was to march down University; right past the children's hospital, so the little ones seeking care could view the festivities. I always found that was a very sweet thing to do, because every child needs to experience that special magic the Santa Claus Parade brings.

With this year's Parade taking place during the run-up to this year's Canadian football Championship, the Game's Organizing Committee decided to design a float celebrating the Contest's 'Centennial Edition' and have it travel the three-and-a-half mile route from Bloor and Christie down to Front and Church. To add some punch, they even opted to have some of the Boatmen's cheerleaders march alongside of it. Personally, I thought football cheerleaders at a children's parade was a little too perverse; given how most football cheerleaders are stereotypically attired. However, since this is Canada, and the old tradition of having a Championship Game Parade on the day before the Big Game was pretty much abolished during the festivities for the 'Grand National Drunk' in 1992, I guess this was their attempt to recapture the glory, and cater it to an all-ages audience.

I couldn't say I blamed the organizers for doing away with the Championship Game Parade. I seem to vaguely recall the last such march during the 1991 Championship in Winnipeg. The Boatmen happened to be playing in the Big Game, and a bunch of Toronto supporters made the trek to the Manitoba capital for the event. The problem was, with most of the attendees who make the trek to the host city, as with any party, the week-long festivities are pretty much an excuse to get completely blotto; hence, the unofficial 'Grand National Drunk' moniker. When the Parade reporter interviewed a bunch of Boatmen fans – who were half in the bag by the time the Saturday afternoon rolled around – who attended the Parade, they made complete drunken asses of themselves. I guess after the embarrassing spectacle, the Organizing Committees of the Championship Game Festival ever since, condemned the public displays of drunkenness into the homes of the nation, and scrapped the Parade altogether. There have been sporadic attempts to bring the march back, but in more family friendly environments. However, I noticed on this year's schedule, there will be a special march of Canadian football fans that had assembled in Toronto on the day before the Big Game, and they would be parading the grand chalice itself. Considering that some of these fans will most likely be bombed by the time the event takes place, I hoped the organizers would conduct breathalyser tests before they were to get their hands on the trophy. The coveted prize was broken by the winning team after its presentation following the 2006 game in Winnipeg. I dreaded a repeat incident by rowdy fans on our downtown streets.

"Penny for your thoughts," Geny asked me, as we were watching the coverage.

I snapped back to reality. "Oh, sorry. I just thinking about the history of Canadian football. The Organizing Committee of the Championship next week has a float slated to be in the Santa Claus Parade, and I was beginning to feel nostalgic."

"That seems a little classless for them to do so. This is supposed to be a children's parade, and they're shilling an event that's catered more to a grown-up audience."

"You'd think that, but the Championship's Organizing Committee is trying to appeal to a broader audience this year; all the way down to the halftime entertainment at the Big Game next Sunday."

"I hate to ask who they have performing, then."

"Well, in a move that's going to upset long-time football fans, they've hired one of the most polarizing acts in today's Canadian music industry."

"Not those hard rockers originally from Alberta who have all the hits that sound exactly the same?"

"Worse, the teen icon from southwestern Ontario that is a male, but his detractors insinuate that he's really female."

Geny fought back the urge to gag. "You have got to be kidding me. They've gotten Jesse Billings to perform at the game? Were the organizers under the influence when they decided upon that?"

"Well, also on the bill is a Canadian folk icon, Gregory Levingston. Maybe the people putting the show together found his stash, and were doing bong hits." My comment brought a big laugh from my dog sitter. "But, I can see what the organizers are trying to do. The long-time fans are getting up there in years, and they want to attract new fans to the product. By advertising a diverse line-up for the halftime entertainment, they can bring in the young fans who will hopefully see how great a game Canadian football is; while at the same time, appeal to the older demographic who have been around for years."

"I guess that's a shrewd marketing strategy, but I still foresee some backlash from the old time fans over Jesse Billings being there."

"Most likely, but the professional league has tried to be modern before with their halftime entertainment, and has gotten backlash for their choice. The most notable was back in 2005 when they got the hottest group in hip hop to perform at halftime for the game in Vancouver. The only thing that lessened the criticism was that the Championship that year turned into a classic that went into overtime. So, hopefully the 100th edition next week will be a game for the ages too. Otherwise, there's going to be a lot of crapping on the product."

~ * * * ~

My friend and I continued to watch the Parade coverage, and marvelled at the creative detail that went into each float. Some of them were based on popular nursery rhymes, others on various aspects of a child's imagination – like Santa's Workshop. All of them featured wondrous designs, complete with the latest animatronics. One might argue the float creators could have previously worked at designing the exhibits and attractions at the big amusement parks in California or Florida. But, for the Parade organizers, they were thankful the designers chose to remain in the Toronto area

I was really starting to relax and enjoy the spectacle when Geny called my attention to something that caught her eye.

"Gary, look," she beckoned. "Someone's in the crowd."

I had to adjust my vision for a bit, but amongst the throngs lining the curb was the all-too-familiar blue and black winter jacket that had taunted me for the past few days. "What the fuck was *he* doing here?" I thought. Whatever the reason, it was not for good intentions. I attempted to analyze the image for the split-second he was on the screen. Like Mr. Lottridge informed me the day before, our suspect was indeed over 6-feet tall, and sported medium-length black hair and moustache. But, he was wearing sunglasses to conceal his eye colour. I couldn't blame him for doing so; the sun came out from the wintery cloud cover to shine down on the proceedings. However, I was able to detect his skin colour, though: Caucasian with a bit of a pigment of melanin to it. It was almost the same skin shade Bennett possessed, but he wouldn't brave the crowds to watch the Parade in person, would he? It was Jessica's voice of doubt in my head that was playing tricks on my mind, I presumed. Regardless, I had to watch for whatever move he was going to make next. However, I didn't know what it would be.

A few moments later, there was pandemonium along the route. One of the floats came careening down the street. It was speeding out of control, at a pace far too fast for a normal parade showpiece. The marchers in front of it, and the spectators on the sidewalk scattered away from the runaway vessel's path. Alas, not everyone was able to get out of the way in time. The float crashed into a fountain situated in the wide median of University Avenue near Dundas, and was stopped in its tracks, but the damage had been done. Numerous marchers who were struck by the out-of-control mobile structure laid injured in the street. The shrieks of horror could be heard from the young and old who bore witness to the accident. The TV cameras panned to the now idle float, and it revealed something I should have known all along: the runaway advertisement that had crashed was the one sponsored by the Championship Organizing Committee.

Within minutes, my phone rang. There were only two people that it might have been calling me, I thought: Jessica or Lt. Davies. Sure enough, it was my superior officer.

"Celdom," he enquired, "where the hell are you?"

"Currently in my living room, sir. I just finished watching the incident at the Santa Claus Parade on the boob tube."

"Well, that's no real help to me, is it? I want you to get off your ass, and prove yourself useful by rounding up Amerson, and getting to the scene ASAP."

"I'm on it, Lieutenant." I acknowledged before hanging up. I turned to my guest, and bore the bad news. "That was Lt. Davies. It's time to make the donuts."

"I understand," Geny nodded, and went to call Siren. "Thank you for the tea and the company while it lasted."

"It's no problem. Come on, I'll drive you home."

My two visitors and I piled into my vehicle, and I dropped them off Geny's quaint abode in Leslieville before I called Jessica and told her we were back on the clock. I picked up my partner at her place in Cabbagetown, and we made our way to the scene of the accident. What we would find out later, the accident was not unintentional.

CHAPTER 11

My partner and I arrived at the site of the accident to find Tamara and the rest of the Forensics team hard at work; combing the area for any possible explanation as to why the Championship float sped out of control on the Parade Route. My first hunch was the vessel was tampered with by our maniacal friend, but I didn't know how he did it. All of the Parade floats were kept in storage at a secret location before being shuttled to the Christie Pits area the morning of the event. So, unless the whack-a-doodle was able to find out where the storage warehouse was, I figured he did his alterations while the showpiece was idling on Bloor West, and he would have had to have been quick about it. In all likelihood, it was probably the former; however, the Parade Organizers had always been good at not revealing the exact location of the warehouse. Our culprit had to have some inside information; a stealth feat all on its own.

"Has your team been able to turn up anything, Hutchins?" I asked the Forensics lead.

"We're still working on it, Detectives."

Jessica presumed, "Considering the float was speeding faster than intended, the accelerator was probably tinkered with, so it would end up sticking."

I disagreed, "That seems too simplistic for our little friend. Most motorized parade floats don't generate enough horsepower to go as fast as this one did. There had to be some sort of booster attached to it."

"That's just a misconception perpetrated by an American satirical animated comedy," Jessica argued.

"I beg to differ."

"Actually," Tamara clarified, "you're both right. Since most of the floats in the Santa Claus Parade are a large size, they use a pontoon boat base. So, if you motorize that with a 50-horsepower engine, you could probably clock in at about 20 miles per hour. That being said, the motor could have been modified to generate more RPMs; thus, increasing the top speed capacity of the vessel."

"So, technically," I concluded, "it could have been either, but that still doesn't explain how the gas pedal ended up getting stuck."

"Hutchins," Scott called out to the Forensics lead. "I think I found something!"

"Excuse me, Detectives." Tamara headed over towards where her teammate was standing. Naturally, Jessica and I didn't want to be left out of the discovery, so we trudged over to him, as well. "What have you got, Harris?"

"I found this discarded in one of the trash cans. It appears to be a remote control device."

"That makes it clear," Jessica deduced. "The float was booby-trapped with a mechanism that would cause its accelerator to stick; thus, speeding the vessel to maximum velocity."

"And the device wasn't activated until our little friend flipped the switch via this remote," I added. "I'm sure if you looked at the undercarriage of the float, you'll find the add-on that caused this."

"Harris," Tamara asked her teammate, "round up a couple of others. I want you to find the rest of the mechanism on the float, and get them analyzed for prints. Like Detectives Amerson and Celdom, I want to find out as much as possible about this cretin, and get him off our streets ASAP. If he's willing to put children's lives in danger, there's no telling what else he might be capable of."

"I'll do the best I can, Hutchins."

"Speaking of which," I interrupted, "Have you gotten the ballistics reports on the previous shootings completed?"

"They're limited because all we've been able to turn up are the bullets, and not the actual weapon itself. But, what we've discovered so far should be on your desk as we speak, Detective Celdom."

"Thanks for that," Jessica appreciated. "Please let us know of anything else that turns up in your investigation."

"That I will, Detective Amerson." Tamara returned her focus to the rest of her staff.

~ * * * ~

Jessica and I began to make our way over to the Division to resume work on the case.

"So much for a presumed quiet Sunday off-duty," I commented.

"I know, I was really looking forward to a day's rest too. Damn this prick for fucking over our plans."

"Don't worry, dear. Hopefully, we'll get this asshole behind bars in due time so we can enjoy some much deserved R&R; presumably before Sunday, so I can enjoy watching the Championship game on TV."

"Speaking of which, aren't the Boatmen playing in Montréal right now?"

I checked my watch and noticed it was almost 4 in the afternoon. "The game should be almost over by now. Let me see if I can get it on the radio."

I turned on my car's audio system, and tuned into the radio station that was covering the match-up.

"It's make or break for the home side, with 47 seconds left," the broadcaster announced, "3rd and 10 for Montréal on the Toronto 23; Boatmen up by 7. The quarterback fades back; he's got a receiver open in the end zone. The QB heaves it downfield... IT'S INCOMPLETE! The

76

Boatmen are going to the Championship Game next week! The Montréal receiver was wide open, but the QB's throw went off the receiver's shoulder pad, and could not come up with the ball. It's a turnover on downs, and all the Toronto QB has to do is kneel down a few times and your Toronto Boatmen will play the winner between Calgary and Vancouver later today in the 100th Canadian Football Championship next Sunday night."

"Well, that was a shocker," I commented. "I thought for sure Montréal was going to be representing the East next week."

"I'm happy for the Boatmen, but it means bad news for us. With the Double Blue playing in the Championship next week, this could possibly give our psychopathic mass-murderer more incentive to kill other fans in the days leading up to the Big Game."

The expression on my face immediately changed to a dire one upon Jessica's presumption. Since the hometown squad would be competing for the league title seven days from now, it would lead to more fans taking in the festivities as the city would be swept up in the attempts to get other Torontonians to climb on the bandwagon. Save for our professional indoor lacrosse franchise – which receives little, if any, recognition compared to the four bigger sports – this was the first time a Toronto-based team would be playing in a championship game in eight years. What's more, said title game would be played here in the Big Smoke; a feat not matched since the Jays played for the baseball championship almost two decades ago. The streets were going to be pandemonium with all of the supporters; which meant a possible shooting gallery for our anti-Canadian football freak who had it in for anyone sporting the Cambridge and Oxford colour combination.

"Gary," my partner attempted to get my attention. "Did you hear what I just said?"

"Oh, he heard you," Karen recognized, as she appeared in my backseat. "He's just coming to the realization that you two are now in quite a pickle."

"And it's a real dill," I snapped too. "If we have any chance of getting this guy, we're going to have to bring in the one guy we both know who can help us in our Canadian football history."

"But, what if it's him to begin with?" Jessica questioned. "He hasn't been completely eliminated from our suspect list yet."

"I know he hasn't. However, he's the best informant we have so far, and if we have him by our side, and the homicides stop; then, we know we'll have the perpetrator amongst us. It'll be risky, but it's the only shot we have right now."

"I hope he doesn't screw us over in the end," Karen cautioned.

"That's the chance I'm willing to take," I said.

Jessica got on her cell phone, and placed a call to our writer friend in Scarborough.

CHAPTER 12

"Will you stop pacing, Gary," Karen begged. "You're going to wear a groove in the floor."

"Yes, please stop," Jessica added. "Bennett will get here when he can."

I was an anxious wreck, and the horrible swill from the vending machine in the Division's Break Room did not help matters. The three of us were awaiting the arrival of our dear friend, in hopes he could help us in our search for the madman who was responsible for not only five deaths, but numerous amounts of injuries over the past few days in our city. With the proclamation that the hometown professional football club would be competing one week from now in the Championship game, my partner and I were concerned that it could lead to even more bloodshed on the streets; more so, since the guy we were after had it in for the Canadian game in general. Mind you, the situation was going to be precarious to begin with, as fans from across the country would be descending into Toronto over the next few days to take in the celebrations. However, since the homicidal maniac had previously targeted fans of the Double Blue, it was believed the team's participation in the Big Game would motivate the psychopath to cause even more damage, and make whatever twisted statement he was attempting to make even louder than before. It was a notion that made me extremely on edge, since we still had only a vague description of who we was, and a suspicion that it could be the person we were waiting to arrive to help us in the investigation.

I was feeling a bit of remorse towards my friend because it was my own partner who insinuated he was the one responsible for all of the carnage in the first place, and based on what few clues we had received so far, he could not be ruled out. However, despite that, I still clung to the faint belief that while he had his share of difficulties as of late, he would not be the type of person who would go on such a rampage on our streets by killing innocent people based solely on their affiliation with the hometown team.

Fifteen minutes later, the man we were waiting for walked into the Division; looking tired and a little irritated.

"You know, Detectives," Phil complained, "I don't mind helping you two out, but asking me to do so when I'm in the midst of attempting to write a 50,000-word novel in 30 days is not good for my creative process."

"We're sorry for that, Bennett," Jessica apologized. "But, we could really use your help on this investigation."

"I don't know how much help I can possibly be, though. Just because I'm writing a detective story, doesn't necessarily mean that I'm all that good with solving a case."

"We understand that," I mentioned, "but, any assistance you could give us would be greatly appreciated."

Phil sighed with a hint of tired frustration, "I'll try my best then. So, what is it you two need help analyzing?"

My partner and I brought our writer friend up to speed on the investigation so far: the shootings at the movie theatre in the Entertainment District the day before followed by the accident at the Santa Claus Parade earlier on in the day. We explained to him the possible connection between those two incidents and the initial homicides on the university campus. Bennett took in all the information, and attempted to figure out any patterns that they might all point towards.

"What's the situation on those caught in the runaway float's path," he asked. "Have any of them succumbed to their injuries?"

"There were quite a few people taken to hospital," Jessica informed. "Thankfully, the accident happened right on Hospital Row, so they didn't have all that far to transport them."

"That's some relief, but still cause of great concern since it was the Championship Organizing Committee's float that was tampered with. If you combine that with yesterday's shooting at the Football Film Festival, and throw in the university shootings for good measure, it would appear that all of these are tied into the Championship Week's Festivities."

"That's what we presumed," I said. "We figured since you're quite a fan of the sport, you might recognize some sort of pattern that might lead us to when and where our suspect might strike next."

"And how many more times he may attempt to do so," Jessica added.

Phil began to think, "It might take a while to go over all of the facts, but I'll see what I'm able to come up with. Does this Division have Wi-Fi? I could set up my Netbook, and start doing some research into the matter."

"I believe it does," I presumed. "You can check and see for certain."

The writer pulled out his mini-laptop computer from his knapsack, and attempted to get a signal. After a few moments, he was successfully connected to the Internet.

"I'm on, Detectives. Now, let me call up my calendar app, so I can note what days each of these incidents occurred. To recap, there were the initial homicides at the university..."

"Yes," Jessica confirmed, "those were back on Thursday night."

He typed the information in, "Two homicides on Thursday night, then the triple homicide at the Entertainment District movie theatre yesterday; followed by the accident at the Santa Claus Parade today."

"Of which," I cited, "it is undetermined if anybody died from yet."

Jessica's phone rang. She excused herself while she took the call; however, I could tell by the expression on her face that it did not bear any good news. Bennett and I looked at each other in confusion, as we waited for it to conclude. Once the phone conversation ended, Jessica informed us of the situation.

"That was the Coroner's Office," she reported. "It turns out five of the injured at the Parade succumbed to their injuries; all of them members of the Boatmen's Cheerleading Squad."

Phil's face took on a look of bewilderment. "Five members? That's quite a few. I would've thought the bulk of them made the trip up to Montréal to lend their support at the Divisional Final."

"I guess a few of them stayed behind to march in the Parade," I mused, "and ended up paying the ultimate price for it."

"That is quite tragic." Phil updated his calendar with the death toll from today.

"It most certainly is," Jessica agreed. "So, that brings the number of people dead since this spree began to an even ten."

"That's far too many football fans killed," I opined. "The only problem is we don't know if this whack job is going to stop at just 10, or if he has any more homicides planned."

Phil thought out loud, "Let me check something here."

"What are you thinking about, Bennett?" I asked.

"I'm just trying to see if there is a certain pattern based on how all of these deaths have come about so far. It's a bit of a hunch, and could be somewhat of a long shot. But, if what I'm thinking is correct, I might be able to determine how many more sacrifices your suspect intends on making."

"It'll be better than what we've been able to come up with at this point," Jessica replied.

The writer went back to work; doing his analysis, while Jessica and I patiently waited. In the meantime, the three of us were paid a visit by someone only two out of the three could see and hear.

"So, this is an odd turn of events," Karen commented. "The person Jessica believes to be the one responsible for all of the mayhem is here helping you two out."

"I still insist he's not the one behind them," I whispered.

"Don't be so sure of your belief, Celdom," Jessica cautioned. "For all we know, this could be a ruse to throw us off his trail."

"You're not willing to drop this, are you, Amerson?"

Karen interrupted, "While I know the two of you have differing opinions, Gary does have somewhat of a point. If Bennett is willing to help the two of you out – albeit, a little hesitant beforehand – then he might not necessarily be the suspect that you're looking for."

"That's my argument, exactly. Why would someone who's killing all of these innocent people assist us in tracking him down?"

"Maybe to lead us on a wild goose chase before squaring off in a final showdown," Jessica considered. "This messed-up psychopath has gotten a little more notoriety with the accident at the Parade earlier. What's not to say he might not get more elaborate by the time his killing spree is over and done with?"

"She does make a case for that," Karen cited. "If this guy is willing to have one of his acts witnessed in front of the general public, he could get even more brazen in his attacks. Athletes, celebrities, politicians; there's no telling who might be next on his hit list."

I took in the weight of the spectre's warning, and it was something that concerned me a great deal. There were going to be a bunch of famous and notable people who would be coming through town for the upcoming Championship; all of them related in some capacity to Canadian football. If our little homicidal maniac was on an anti-Canadian game crusade, there would be a potential smorgasbord for him to feast upon over the next few days in his bid to have his sadistic voice heard. Should he be more flamboyant in his slayings, it would be another public relations fiasco for the police, and both Jessica and I would be in the scrutinizing crosshairs; although, since my track record has been less than stellar, I would be the one taking the brunt of the criticism. The calls for my removal from the Toronto P.D. would become so loud, everyone in the country would want my head. I was becoming lost in my own thoughts when I was brought back to reality by the writer working at Jessica's desk.

"Uh, Detective Celdom," Phil queried. "Are you alright there?"

"Sorry, Bennett. I was thinking about everything that could happen if we're not able to catch this guy promptly. He's already killed ten people – five of which were at the Parade earlier. I just don't want any high profile people to find themselves in his deadly path."

"That's understandable. There's going to be so many people attending all of the events over the next few days, there could be any number of locales where he might strike next."

"Such as?"

"Well, you have kids' events going on down at Yonge-Dundas Square, the zip line over at City Hall, all of the team-themed parties and concerts in and around the Convention Centre; although, the Edmonton boosters are doing their events at the hotel across from City Hall. There's the Player Awards up at that recital hall beside the downtown university stadium, and of course the University Championship on Friday night and the professional Championship next Sunday, both of which are at the domed stadium. It's a pretty full schedule of events all around the downtown core."

"And that is what's worrying us," Jessica chimed in. "If you're able to pick out this pattern, like you say you might be able to do, then we can try to nip him in the bud before it gets worse."

"Well, Detective Amerson, I think I might have been able to figure something out. You said he's been targeting Argo fans throughout his entire carnage, correct?"

"That seems to be the common bond between all of the dead, so far."

"Well, I could be wrong on this, but it would appear that the killing pattern is also an ominous homage to them."

I was confused by Phil's statement. "How can someone who's offing all of these Double Blue supporters be honouring the club they support at the same time?"

"That's something that's confused me too, Detective Celdom, but this makes the most logical sense. Check this out, next Sunday will be the 100th edition of the Canadian professional football Championship, right?"

"Yes, but, what does that have to do with our psychopath?"

"Well, if you were to break it down into groups of 10 championships, you'll notice a pattern with disturbing similarities began to emerge."

My partner and I peered over the writer's shoulder and squinted at his Netbook's screen. He had called up a list of all the prior Championship victors, and cross-referenced it to a spreadsheet that broke the list down into groups of 10. It was revealed within that list, how many times the Boatmen had hoisted the prized chalice within the Championship's history; fifteen times in all. However, when Phil segmented the list, it unveiled the number of times the Double Blue had won the trophy within every 10 editions the Championship had been played.

"Now," Phil surmised, "if you figure each group of 10 championships coincides with a certain day on the calendar..."

"Oh my dear God," Jessica announced in astonished horror. "It exactly matches the number of deaths that have transpired so far."

"With the Dawkins and Simmons murders as the initial day of the pattern," I added.

"Exactly, Detectives. That is why your madman is paying a bloody homage to the team he detests with a passion. Granted, the number of deaths he committed today was randomly coincidental to it matching the pattern, but all the same."

"Be it as it may," Jessica remarked, "at least now we have an idea of when he'll strike next, and how many targets will be on his scope."

"Yes," I nodded, "but, the problem is, we don't know where those strikes will be yet. Bennett, based on this established pattern, when are the next slayings scheduled for?"

"Let me compute this for you." Phil typed away before announcing the answer. "According to this, if the pattern stays true, he plans to kill two people this coming Thursday, another couple of people on Friday, and one more sacrifice on Saturday. So, you'll have a couple of days to rally your fellow officers to try and track down this sick freak."

"That could change, though," Jessica mentioned. "The Boatmen are playing in the Championship next week, so there's the potential for a 16th body should it come to that."

"They beat Montréal?" Phil gave an astonished look. "I didn't think they'd get the 'W' against such a dominant veteran squad. What about the Western Divisional Final? Has that been decided yet?"

I checked my watch, and saw that it was approaching 7:15 in the evening.

"It might be late in that game," I pronounced. "Unfortunately, we don't have a TV or a radio in here where we could find out the results."

"No worries about that, Detective Celdom. I can find out online. Fortunately, I was already on the Canadian Pro Football website when I was calling up the original list of previous Championship winners, so I'll just go back to the main page to see what the score is."

The next thing I knew, Phil called up a Flash animation plug-in on his web browser that would show the progress of the game up to that point; listing all of the offensive drives Calgary and Vancouver had, team statistics, and scoring plays. I had to admit, I was astonished at how the technology had become in today's information age. I remembered years ago when I was

86

growing up that when it came to watching hockey games, all you were able to watch on the television was one game at a time, and they wouldn't give you any out-of-town scores until the intermissions. Nowadays, all of the score updates can happen "on-the-fly" and the information is passed on almost instantaneously. It's remarkable how much things had advanced over the years.

"It looks like Vancouver just scored a touchdown to put them within 5 of Calgary with 59 seconds left," Phil announced. "This late in the game, they might try an on-side kick to try and get the ball back for one last scoring attempt."

"That type of play usually doesn't work, does it?" I posed.

"Normally, it doesn't; however, a few weeks back, the Ti-Cats attempted such a play late in the game against this same Calgary side on a snowy evening in southern Alberta, and were able to pull it off. The only problem was the Black and Gold would eventually lose the game when they botched the snap on a game-winning field goal attempt."

"That must have been heartbreaking for you," Jessica empathised, "since I know how much of a fan you are of them."

"Not as much as their final game of the regular season here in Toronto. Here they were, needing to win to make the playoffs; down by as much as 15 points in the 3rd quarter, and they come back to tie it up late in the game. It looked like the game would go into overtime, but the Boatmen come storming back down the field, and end up kicking a 51-yarder to win and knocking their rivals from down the Q.E.W. out of post-season contention."

"That surely must have made you upset," Jessica probed. I shot her a stern look because I knew she had just asked a leading question.

"I wouldn't say upset, but I was disappointed. The Ti-Cats had so much promise going into this season; only to fall flat on their face. But I put the blame squarely on the coaching staff. Their big off-season acquisition at quarterback was spotty on his accuracy, and our defence and special teams let us down constantly. Sure, it would have been great had they made the playoffs, but I don't think they would have lasted long once they got there."

The writer turned his attention back to his portable computer's screen. Vancouver was setting up for the short kick-off attempt. Should the ball travel at least ten yards, they would have the opportunity to retrieve it. However, should an opposing player from Calgary get to the ball before one of the Vancouver players did – or, if the kick failed to travel the necessary distance – then the team representing the southern Alberta city would gain possession; thus, solidifying the contest for them, and sending them east for the Championship game. As with all onside kick attempts, the booted ball sailed high into the air, while both teams jockeyed for position. But, for the defending champions, their bid for a comeback fell short, as a Calgary player caught the ball before being tackled immediately.

"Well, that pretty much settles it," Phil pronounced. "Next week, it will be Calgary versus Toronto down at the dome, with the league title on the line."

"That's a bit of a shock," I opined. "Both of the favourites ended up losing their Divisional Finals at home."

"Have Calgary and Toronto ever played for the Championship before?" Jessica asked the writer.

"Twice, actually. The first was back in 1971 on a rain-soaked field in Vancouver. The Boatmen were threatening to score the winning touchdown, but ended up fumbling on the Calgary 3-yard line.

"That must have left a sour taste in the city's mouth," she presumed.

"It did, but the Boatmen would extract their revenge exactly two decades later on a bitterly cold day in Winnipeg. The owners of the Double Blue back then assembled a star-studded line-up that would defeat Calgary and give Toronto their second title since that ill-fated contest on the West Coast."

"So, with all of that history," I questioned, "it should make for an entertaining game, right?"

"Shit, it should make for an entertaining week. With Calgary playing in the Championship, there is the potential to turn this city into one big hootenanny; just like it was back in 1948."

"What happened back then?" Jessica probed.

"That was the year Calgary played in their first Championship game. Ironically, it was right here in Toronto, up at the midtown university, against Ottawa. That year, a bunch of fans from southern Alberta made the trek across the country for the game. Their crowning achievement, and I kid you not, was riding a horse into the lobby of that big hotel across from Union Station."

"Are you serious, Bennett?" I doubted. "They rode an actual live horse into the hotel lobby?"

"Yes, they sure did. Since then, it has been a tradition every time Calgary has played in the Big Game. But, even when they're not playing for the Championship, at some point during the week leading up to Sunday, a bunch of Calgary hospitality people will throw a big outdoor pancake breakfast."

"Come to think of it," I recollected, "I believe I heard somewhere that was going to be down at City Hall late Saturday morning. That's going to be pretty brazen of them, since the two cities will be squaring off for the league title later on in the weekend."

"Hopefully," Jessica mused, "cooler heads will prevail, and there won't be any incident. We have enough problems as it is with a homicidal maniac on the streets. The last thing we need is a bunch of drunk, rival football fans brawling in Nathan Phillips Square."

"Especially," Phil noted, "since the Edmonton hospitality faction is hosting their annual Championship breakfast event in the hotel right across the street from the Calgary outdoor one, and it is rumoured that they serve Screwdrivers in place of orange juice at the Edmonton meal."

"We better free up some room in the Drunk Tank. We'll be trying to get a few people to sober up in there Saturday afternoon."

Phil laughed, "I don't think it will be that bad. For the most part, fans who travel to the Championship's host city are pretty civil. Sure, they might enjoy a 'wobbly pop' too many, but they've all come to town to party, and have a good time."

"Just as long as the local crazies don't use it as an opportunity to trash the city post-game, we should be fine," I cautioned.

Phil yawned, "Is there anything else you'd like of me, Detectives? It's getting late, and I didn't get much sleep this weekend."

"No, I think that's pretty much it, Bennett," Jessica appreciated. "Thank you again for coming down, and helping us out on such short notice."

"No problem. I hope the info I have provided will help lead you towards the guy you're looking for."

"Come on, Bennett," I offered. "I'll drive you home. We can talk about our respective novel projects."

"Thank you, Detective Celdom." Phil gathered his things. "I would like that. Again, it's always a pleasure to see you, Detective Amerson."

I grabbed my coat, and Jessica gave me a "Find out what you can about him" look; to which, I returned a "Give it up" glare. I turned to my friend, and showed him to my car. I could tell my partner was still not convinced of Phil's innocence, but since I could feel Karen's presence following me towards the garage, I was sure that somehow I was going to be needled about it all the way to Scarborough and back.

CHAPTER 13

When I've been hanging out with my writing compatriot in the recent past, it had been a stress-free experience. It was the feeling one had when two friends were sharing some friendly banter and enjoying each other's company. However, this particular evening, there was an underlying tension in the air; the same kind the two of us felt when we endured the hostage situation at the fan convention a mere three months before. I looked over at the writer as I drove, and he glanced back at me; both of us sharing a nervous chuckle. One of us had to speak in a bid to break the ice. I figured I should be the one to take the initiative.

"So," I enquired, "how are you faring in the novel writing challenge this month?"

"It's been a bit of a rough go, but I was able to crack 30K on the subway Saturday afternoon."

"Oh yeah, that was this weekend. Was it a big turnout this year?"

"Not really. Because of the partial closure last weekend, they had to push it back to this one. Then, they had to change it to Saturday because of the Santa Claus Parade today. If it wasn't for the Halfway Party being held the night before, more people might have shown up at Downsview to write."

"Judging by the sound of your voice, it sounds like you did both events, and ended up paying for it."

"Am I ever; I didn't get home from the restaurant out in Bloor West Village until 11:30 Friday night. Then, I had the bright idea to work on my novel for a bit when I got home. Boy, was that a mistake. I think I only got a few hours' sleep before I had to be up and out the door, so I could meet up with everyone at Downsview for 1 o'clock Saturday afternoon."

"Yeah, it sounds like you're exhausted. Hopefully, a good night's sleep will set you back on track."

"That is if I *can* sleep." Phil yawned.

"Something wrong, buddy?"

Phil nuzzled into his heat. "I just have a lot of shit on my mind lately."

I stammered, "You know, Phil, if you ever wanted to talk to someone about things, I'm just a phone call away."

There was a pregnant pause in the vehicle.

"Bennett," I cleared my throat "Are you alright over there?"

The next thing I heard was the writer snoring, as he slept in the passenger seat. I breathed a nervous sigh because I now was left with some doubts in my mind. The snoring was drowned out by a critical voice from the backseat.

"Well, that was all for naught," Karen quipped. "You were about to get somewhere, and he ends up falling asleep on you."

"I'm guessing Jessica sent you to keep an eye on us?"

"Your girlfriend had no part in this."

"Then, why are you in my backseat?"

"Gary, as much as you don't want to admit it, there is a possible suspect sleeping beside you. Now, I don't know if he's your psychopath or not, but until you have a definitive 'yay or nay,' you cannot rule him out entirely."

"Let me ask you something then: Was there ever a time – during your tenure in Edmonton – where you were put in a situation where one of your best friends and confidants was accused of a serious offence that you knew in your heart they were innocent of?"

"Not really, no. Well, there was my best friend, Tammy, who was accused of shoplifting drug store cosmetics, but this is different."

"It was still a crime, Karen. But, you still believed she didn't do it."

"Yes, I did. But, petty theft is nothing compared to multiple homicides. These are serious offences he is possibly responsible for."

"I am fully aware of that. However, if he really is the one we are looking for, then why did he help Jessica and me in determining the pattern?"

"Yes, but he only told you *when* they would occur. He never gave you an idea of where they would exactly happen, nor if he's even seen the suspect. Have you even shown him the images from the security cam footage?"

"Jessica hasn't shown them to him either."

"Nevertheless, it is something you need to bring to Bennett's attention; if not to compare him as a suspect, then as a possible eyewitness. Maybe he knows the guy you are looking for from some other capacity. Shit, he's got his Netbook with him. Get him to look some information up."

I didn't feel like arguing with my former fiancée's ghost with my friend sleeping beside me, but what she said had merit. While we were at the Division, we should have asked the writer about the guy we had on tape. What's more, there was additional footage of our suspect at the Parade this afternoon; something we needed to get from the Parade broadcaster, and add it to our existing files. It was a lapse in judgment on both our parts, but it was something the two of us should explore in the upcoming days. Especially since, according to the perceived pattern, there would be three days until our assailant would strike again. Alas, there was nothing I could do while Phil was snoozing except continue to drive him to his abode, like I promised. Damn, my current string of bad luck.

~ * * * ~

We eventually pulled up in front of Phil's apartment building, but he was still snoring away. I attempted to rouse him awake by nudging him. To which, I got him bemoaning, "Not now, Amy. I'm not in the mood." It was a comment that puzzled me. Amy was my friend's former flame, but they had broken up this past May, I presumed it was a flashback from when they were still together.

I nudged my friend again, and uttered, "Get up, Bennett. We're back at your place."

The writer woke up groggy from his slumber, "Oh, did I sleep the entire drive back? Sorry about that, Gary."

"That's alright. You had a full weekend, and needed to catch up on your rest."

Phil gathered his wares, "Thanks again for driving me back to my place."

"Not a problem, buddy. It was the least I could do after you helped us out tonight."

"My pleasure." Phil got out of my car, "Don't be afraid to contact me if you need any more help."

I was going to end it there, but I felt a ghostly smack against the back of my head. "Actually, Phil, there is one more thing I was wondering if you could help me out with."

"What is it, Gary?"

"I meant to show you while you were down at the Division. We were able to get a screen cap of the guy we're on the trail of. If I were to email you a copy, do you think you might be able to help us place him from something football-related you may have seen online?"

"I could try, but I can't guarantee that I'll be successful."

"I know it might be difficult to pull off, but anything you find would help the investigation a great deal."

The writer stood and thought about it for a bit. I could tell he was becoming agitated because he was tired, and I kept asking him for all of these favours. I wouldn't have been surprised if he fired back and criticized

94

me for not doing what I was paid to do, but eventually he relented. He reached into his knapsack, pulled out a pen and a scrap of paper, and wrote something down.

Phil handed me the slip of paper. "Here's my email address. Send me the screen cap, and I'll see what I can find. It might not be for a bit, but I'll see what I can do."

"Thank you; this is a big help. I'll email you the image when I get back to the office. Have a good night, and I hope to hear from you soon."

The tiredness emanated in Phil's voice, "Goodnight, Gary. Have a safe drive back."

I drove off, and saw my friend head into the building in my rear view mirror. I thought I would have a nice quiet drive back to the Division; however, because of my extra passenger in the backseat, I would end up having a conversation with them during my journey.

"I think you're making a mistake here," Karen worried.

"You mean by getting Bennett to help us further?"

The sarcasm dripped from her voice, "No, Gary, for getting him to scratch your ass. Of course I mean getting him to help you ID the suspect. That's supposed to be the responsibility of yourself and Jessica; not the guy who could possibly be the one you've been after all along."

"I know it's an unconventional approach, but he is more tapped into the online world when it comes to Canadian football talk. I thought he might be able to find out via his various avenues if there have been any hateful sentiments posted on any of the message boards he frequents."

"Or, he could be leading you two on a wild goose chase. If he is the guilty party, you and Jessica will be spinning your wheels while more innocent lives are lost."

I grew angry, "Oh, for the love of… you two women aren't going to drop this, are you?"

"And you have a better idea of who the real killer is? Face it, Gary, all you have right now is a description of the suspect."

"Oh, so you're saying because Jessica has a perceived positive ID that I should haul Bennett in, and lock him up? I'm not going to do that, Karen; not to my best friend."

The spectre threw up her ghostly hands in frustration, "Fine then, do it your way then. But, let me ask you this: How do you think your superior officer is going to react when he finds out you have a civilian assisting you on this case?"

I suddenly felt a dread begin to wash over me. While the public assisting the police when providing witness accounts is encouraged, having them do our investigative work was frowned upon. We were paid to do our jobs, and here I was, outsourcing some of my duties. If I were found out, I would be reprimanded once again, and since I was skating on thin ice to begin with, I could have been fined or suspended once again. I had just gotten back from a two-week ordered leave on the Saunders case a month ago. Being told to sit out for another fortnight so soon after returning would be a noticeable mark on my record, and could lead the higher ups to ratchet up their efforts to force me into retirement. That was something I wasn't ready to do yet, so I had to be extra cautious in handling this.

I chose my words carefully, "You're right, Karen. I'm taking a big risk in getting Bennett to help us. Hell, I'm surprised Jessica and I weren't reprimanded when we brought him into the Division to analyze the pattern."

"Yes, you two were lucky that you got away with it. However, if you're caught sending evidence out to be analyzed, you might not be as fortunate. Then, the shit will hit the fan, and you – and maybe Jessica – will be suspended. What good will it do if one, if not both, of you are told to sit this one out?"

"Not very productive, I would imagine."

"Exactly. That's why if you go through with this, you'll have to make sure you cover your tracks to minimize any possible backlash that might come of it, should you be found out."

"If that's the case, I better see if I have a USB Flash drive at my place that I could transfer the image onto, and send it from home. It'll be tricky since the computers at the Division are heavily monitored, but I'll see what I can do."

The rest of the drive back to the Division would prove to be an unnerving one, and with just cause. I was in a situation where I could find myself back in the crosshairs of my superiors. It was not something I wanted to endure again so soon, but I felt if I was going to find this guy, I needed help. The only problem was, the person I was asking assistance from, might have been – in my partner's eyes – the one I should've been looking for all along.

CHAPTER 14

"Celdom, Amerson," a voice bellowed. "Get your asses in here right now!"

The command was uttered by a very agitated Lt. Davies, who ordered my partner and me into his office. It was a couple of days after I asked Bennett to help me out in identifying our assailant. I was able to sneak the image of him onto a spare USB Flash drive I had lying around my house, brought it home, and emailed it to my writing compatriot in hopes something might have clicked with him. I had a sinking feeling that an audit of the computer systems in the Division discovered the illegal file copy.

"Yes, Lieutenant," Jessica acknowledged our superior officer. I closed the door behind us.

"I just got a call from our IT Department. You know that screen capture from the security cam footage you obtained last week?"

"You mean, from the coffee shop near the university, sir?" I enquired.

"That would be the one, Celdom. Apparently, the IT guys have it on record that the image was transferred onto a removable storage device from Amerson's computer. You two wouldn't happen to know anything about this, would you?"

I didn't need to look beside me; I could feel the cold like dagger stare from my partner. I had been found out of my actions, and now both Jessica and I were being called out onto the carpet of it. I took a deep breath, and decided to come clean.

"I did it, Lieutenant," I confessed. "I was the one who copied the file onto a USB Flash drive from Amerson's computer."

"Please tell me this was to work on the case from your home, Detective."

"It was in part, sir, but I had emailed it to someone who I believed could determine who it was from my home computer."

"And you didn't think of asking for permission first before doing so?"

I hung my head, and admitted, "It was a lapse in judgment, sir, and I take full responsibility for it."

Lt. Davies rubbed his eyes, as if to alleviate a sudden migraine. "Just out of curiosity, Detective Celdom, who was it that you emailed the file to?"

"A friend of mine, Mr. Phil Bennett of Scarborough. He's been assisting us in the investigation."

My superior spoke with a calm tone, but I could see his face turn red with anger. "I see. You're dismissed, Detective Amerson, but I want to have a word with your 'partner' alone."

"Thank you, Lieutenant." Jessica said. She headed out of the office, and closed the door behind her.

What followed was one of the biggest dressing downs I had ever received. I don't think it ranked as bad as the one I received following the hostage situation, but it was high on the list.

~ * * * ~

Jessica made her way back to her desk, and was met by a familiar ghostly figure.

"I warned him this was going to happen," Karen shook her head.

"I don't know what possessed him to do this."

"Apparently, he thought that since Bennett was tapped into the Canadian football online community, the writer might have been able to turn up some information that could have helped you identify the lowlife who's responsible for all the carnage."

Jessica sighed, "Celdom's still hanging onto the belief that his friend didn't do it, is he?"

"It would appear that way. He's letting his friendship cloud his better judgment."

"What's your take on the situation? Do you think Bennett is behind all of these heinous crimes?"

"Honestly, I'm not sure. He does seem like a nice guy. Does he have his problems? Of course, he does. Just look at everything he's gone through in his life. If that isn't cause for someone to snap, then I wouldn't blame him for lashing out; he does have the build to cause some physical harm. However, he has kept it together for the most part, and hasn't resorted to taking it out on others. At least, not yet, from as far as we've been able to determine."

"That is, until possibly now. Maybe all this novel writing stuff has started to wear him down. Gary says Bennett has been doing this for three years, but hasn't gotten published yet. It could be a possibility that the writer is putting extra pressure on himself to get his work out there for public viewing."

Karen mused, "Hmm, that's an interesting theory. Bennett did say that he had a lot of things on his mind as of late. Perhaps that's one of them."

"And another might be all of these murders."

"Possibly, but until we're able to really pick his brain, we won't know for certain."

"How do you suggest I do that? With Gary sticking up for him, I might have to do this behind his back, and I don't want to turn my partner more against me. It'll be bad enough that he'll be in a bit of a foul mood once he gets out of the Lieutenant's office."

"If that's the case, you'll have to do your investigative work undercover. Wait until Gary's relaxing at home, then head on out to Scarborough yourself, and start snooping around Bennett's apartment building. But, do it in your own car. While there is the Anti-Violence Unit patrolling his neighbourhood, he knows your usual unmarked squad car. You don't want to tip him off on what you're up to."

"I might just do that. Thanks for the tip."

I came out of Lt. Davies' office, and like the girls had presumed, I was not sporting a smile on my face. I let out an agitated sigh, grabbed my coat, and began to storm out. I was almost out of the Bullpen when Jessica caught my attention.

"Celdom, wait," she called to me. "What was the verdict? How bad are you being reprimanded?"

I fumed, "Let me summarize it for you, Amerson. Because of my actions, I get to cool my heels again for another two weeks because not only am I off the case, I have been suspended once again."

"But, what about Bennett? Did you tell the Lieutenant about...?"

I blew up at my partner, "Look, Amerson, I have fucking had it with you and your accusations about Bennett being a suspect. So, you know what? Do what you want to do. If you want to bring his ass in and lock him up, then by all means, knock yourself out. But, don't think that for one Goddamn second that I'm going to let that ride."

I stormed out of the Division, and left Jessica and Karen standing there. I could tell that my girlfriend was disheartened by my behaviour, but I had enough of the entire investigation. I still knew in my heart that my best friend was innocent, but I could not get either of the women in my life to believe me. One thing I did know, if I was to protect Phil I had to act fast. I knew Jessica would be staking out his apartment building in due time, and the minute he stepped out to either a therapy session -- or to head over to the grocery store to buy milk -- she would scoop him up and throw him into holding. I couldn't let her do that to him; not now, not ever. I climbed into my car, and took a second to compose myself. I remembered that Bennett was home alone in the afternoon. After my realization, it took a few minutes before I devised my solution. I pulled out of the Division's parking lot, called my friend up on my hands-free device for my cell phone, and began to put my plan into place.

CHAPTER 15

A couple of hours later, I found myself driving eastbound on Highway 401 through Durham Region with my pet husky in the backseat, and Phil riding shotgun. I felt bad for taking my writing friend away from his natural environment, but it was the only way I knew how to protect him from Jessica or any other member of the Division. On the flipside, I thought the time away might do him good. It would give him the opportunity to relax, think about whatever was troubling him, and work on his novel writing challenge project.

"So, where is it exactly we are going to again?" he enquired.

"We're going to my cottage up on Rice Lake, east of Bailieboro."

"That will be nice. I have an uncle who lives closer to South Monaghan; near the banks of the Otonabee River. But, I thought you said you closed it up for the winter last month during Thanksgiving weekend."

"I did, but since this was on a spur of the moment, I swung by a hardware store and picked up a backup generator that should last us for a couple of days. When did you say you wanted to be back?"

"Preferably Saturday." Phil rethought his words. "Actually, to maximize this 'alone time', we should come back Saturday night, and you could maybe drop me off at the Overnight writing session venue, if it's not too much trouble, please?"

"I can do that, if you'd like. There's nothing wrong with that."

Phil settled in and watched the landscape zoom by. "Thanks again for the offer. I can certainly use the time away."

"Oh yes, those things you said you had on your mind. Do you care to talk about it?"

"There are just a lot of things I'm dealing with right now."

"Are they related to your writing, or are they more of a personal nature?"

"Oh, they're all personal, Gary, and I think it's beginning to affect my writing. I'm having a tough time trying to concentrate this November."

"I hope it's nothing to do with Jessica and me asking you to help out with the investigation. If so, I apologize for causing the distraction."

"It's not that. It's just some shit that I've been trying to sort out since the beginning of October."

'Trying to sort out since the beginning of October'? That means Phil had been troubled by this for a few weeks now. This almost assures that he is not responsible for all of the recent murders, or does it? Phil never struck me as the type who would lash out at others physically. Sure, he may have had thoughts about wishing harm upon others; maybe he has said heated words in the past that may have contained idle threats. But, to actually raise his hand in anger or hatred, that doesn't seem like his nature. I wanted to probe further to find out for certain; however, that would have me falling into my partner's line of thinking – something I did not want to adhere to because I still thought my friend was better than that.

I was about to ask the writer to be for certain when my cell phone went off. I got Phil to screen the call for me.

"It's Jessica," he reported.

I let out a disenchanted groan. "Could you do me a favour, and turn off my phone for me, please?"

"But, she might be calling about the case."

"Yes, but I'm officially off of it, and have been suspended for the next two weeks. It's out of my hands, and I don't want to think about it. Right now, I just want to get away from it all, and relax for a couple of days out of the city."

"Your wish is my command." Phil held the 'Off' button, and powered down my phone.

"Thanks. Now, without many distractions, you could just let the words flow as you write."

"Indeed, they will. I think the quality has really suffered this year because of the lack of focus."

"Hey now, you're further ahead than I am. With all of the recent cases I've been assigned, I doubt I'll be able to reach half of the necessary 50K by the end of the month."

"Well, with us at your cottage, we'll both be able to punch up our respective word counts."

"I sure hope so."

~ * * * ~

An hour later, we pulled up to my cottage. It was not very big, but it's ample enough for me, Benny, and maybe one guest. I haven't had the opportunity to invite Jessica up since we rarely got time off from work at the same time. I hoped one day I would be able to host my girlfriend for a summer weekend, so she could relax, sit on the back patio with a cool beverage, and enjoy the scenery. I always did whenever I was up here.

I showed Phil to his room, and helped him get settled before I opted to take Benny for a walk, since he'd been cooped up in my car for a couple of hours. Much to my surprise, my friend decided to join us. I guess he wanted to stretch his legs, too. As we strolled along the lakeside gravel roadway, we talked about various things.

"Do you like Toronto?" the writer asked me.

"It's alright. Why do you ask?"

"Oh, I was wondering if you've ever thought about living somewhere else should the opportunity arise."

"Well, I did think about moving out west years ago."

"Let me guess, out to Edmonton, right?"

"Yes, I was considering transferring out there when I was going to marry Karen. I even had my request in for the relocation. But, when she was tragically gunned down on our wedding day, I revoked my application, and opted to stay here in Ontario.

"Did you ever regret changing your mind and staying?"

"What do you mean?"

Phil explained, "Well, I mean, do you think the city has gotten worse over the years?"

"Phil, any city is bound to get worse over time. With the increase in population density, the proliferation of guns – whether they be legal or illegal in Western culture – along with other crime aspects, and the emergence of tough economic problems, there are bound to be some undesired aspects cropping up in the modern era."

"Duly noted, but knowing how the city has become over, say, the past 20 years or so, do you find it as something that disheartens you?"

"Admittedly, it does. I prefer a more simplistic time when there weren't as many people roaming the streets. Don't get me wrong, some of the changes have been for the better, but other aspects, not as much."

"I'm guessing in the latter instance, you mean all of those condo buildings down along the waterfront."

"Exactly. Those things are such an eyesore. Then again, some may argue the elevated portion of the Gardiner isn't any better."

"You trade one bit of ugly city planning with another. It seems like one can't win worth trying."

"It doesn't look like it. What about you? Have you ever thought about moving anywhere out of Toronto?"

I could tell Phil was hesitant, but gave his answer. "I don't know. For a while now I've been thinking about getting out of the big city and into somewhere a little smaller."

"Like Hamilton, for example? You know, so you wouldn't have a 2-hour commute each way to go to a Ti-Cat game."

Phil chuckled, "I don't have to worry about that until 2014. Not until the new stadium opens."

"Speaking of which, have they announced where they're playing next year yet? They've been dragging their heels on that for a long time."

"Actually, they unveiled it a couple of days ago. They'll be temporarily playing up in Guelph."

"They don't have a suitable stadium up there, do they?"

"They don't, but there is a small one at the university up there. The Ti-Cats will expand it with temporary bleachers. However, it will be smaller than Ivor Wynne was by about 15,000 seats."

"That is going to make for some cramped quarters, and some irate fans who will want to commute up from Hamilton for the games."

"It already has, but this is a one year fix while Ivor Wynne is torn down, and the new stadium is built. The team wanted to play next year as close to the Steel City as possible, and when they couldn't reach an agreement with the university in west Hamilton, Guelph was the next best option; which, I guess is good in the end. At least the fans won't be commuting for over an hour, just to get to the university stadium in London."

"Had that been the case, it would've been too bad that you're not still with Amy. You could have stayed at her place while you attended the games there."

Phil smirked, "Yeah. That would have been nice."

I could tell I was treading close to territory that was making my friend uncomfortable, so I decided to drop the subject. I presumed he still wasn't over his girlfriend from last year. The two had met through the annual novel writing challenge, and it blossomed into a long-distance relationship with Phil still in Scarborough and Amy a two-hour commute away in the Forest City. Things were going along well for the two aspiring writers until last May when the two ended their union, with Amy citing personal issues on her end. Phil held onto the hope that they would reunite one day, but it ended up not to be. The two met up a couple of months ago to attend an exhibit at the major art gallery downtown; however, relations were strained to the point where any chance for reconciliation seemed slim to none. To the best of my knowledge, they had not spoken to each other since. It was an unfortunate circumstance because Phil appeared to be crazy about her, and I believed he still carried a torch for the lass from London, Ontario.

~ * * * ~

Once Benny had enough exercise, and did his biological business, the three of us returned to my cottage. I fired up the generator, and began to start cooking dinner; while Phil grabbed a quick shower. Thankfully, I bought some groceries before I picked up my writing compatriot, so the three of us wouldn't starve as we were in virtual hiding. I just hoped Jessica didn't try to call Phil in a bid to lure him out of his apartment, and ended up getting his roommate instead. That would have completely blown our cover. However, I'm not sure if the writer left a note explaining where he was going. All I told him over the phone when I called him up was, 'How would you like to get away for a couple of days?' He leapt at the opportunity, and then we were on our way.

I ended up preparing a simplistic meal of 'beans and franks' for Phil and me, and heated up some extra wieners for Benny to dine on along with his usual kibble. It wasn't much, but it satisfied all of us. I promised to make some homemade beef stew for dinner the next night to make up for the lackluster sustenance. It was a suggestion that pleased my friend so much he enthusiastically offered to help chop the vegetables for the slow-cooked creation. If it wasn't for the fact that we still had to do the dishes and pots from the first night's dinner, he would have wanted to get started on it right away. It brought a smile onto my face that the tense situation back home for both of us had been all but forgotten. I breathed a sigh of relief, and enjoyed the relaxed atmosphere in the Kawarthas.

After we finished cleaning up, Phil suggested the two of us get to work on our literary projects; to which, I agreed. We would fire up our respective laptop computers, plugged in the USB Flash drives that housed our individual works-in-progress, and began to type the night away. We even threw down a few word sprints – where we raced to write as many words as possible within a set time frame – for good measure. The writer would beat me in all of them, but I would come close to defeating him a couple of times. We would write away into the wee hours of the morning, until I started to get drowsy. By the time I checked the clock, it ended up being 2 o'clock Thursday morning. I suggested we call it a night, and start fresh in the morning. Phil agreed with a yawn and we prepared to sleep in the cottage on the shores of Rice Lake. As I was lying in my bed away from home, I couldn't help but think about the case I had been thrown off of. I wondered if Jessica had any luck in tracking down our mystery psychopath, and how long it would be until he was captured. Until then, I worried about the safety of not only the Boatmen fans he appeared to have been targeting, but all of visiting fans from out-of-town.

CHAPTER 16

As the two days passed I began to feel re-energized. I presumed the rest from the hustle and bustle from the Division was what the doctor ordered. It appeared the time away did Phil some good too, as we both made strides on our respective novel writing projects. I figured by the time Saturday morning came around, my writing compatriot had written close to 10,000 words. I ended up logging a good 8,000 words of my own; a feat not too shabby for an old fart like me, I thought. I still doubted I would be able to make 50,000 by the end of the month, but at least we both made a lot of progress towards our respective goals. As a reward for our efforts, I decided to cook us both a hearty breakfast of bacon and eggs. It was a meal that awoke my friend's senses, as I could see him act like he was floating on air; the aroma drawing him towards the kitchen.

"Good morning," I greeted with a grin. "Did my cooking wake you up?"

Phil laughed, "I had to make sure I wasn't dreaming. I haven't had bacon and eggs in a very long time."

"Well, you're not dreaming. This is real maple-smoked bacon and 'Grade A' Canadian eggs that I'm frying up."

"My mouth is watering already."

"I'm surprised you don't make them more often."

"Are you kidding? Have you seen the price of bacon nowadays? You're looking at close to $4 for a decent looking pound. Plus, I have to be careful about eggs in general because of the cholesterol content."

"You have problems with your cholesterol levels?"

"I do, but it's not because my LDL is too high; it's my HDL that's too low. Because of that, I have to take medication to rectify it; one 5-milligram tablet a day at dinner."

"That sucks. How long have you had to take these supplements?"

"For about five years now, just after I was diagnosed with Type-II diabetes."

I was concerned for my friend. "But, you're alright now, right?"

"Oh, yeah. I do my regular blood tests, and I do my best to try and watch my weight. However, it is still a pain in the ass."

"I can imagine it would be. So, you want me to give you just bacon?"

"No, no, I can still have eggs, but I should limit them to a maximum of two. Anything more than that is pushing it."

"Two eggs it is then. How do you like them?"

"Over easy, please."

I prepared our breakfasts to our orders: two eggs and four strips of bacon each for the writer and myself; while my pet husky was given three strips of the maple-smoked pork to gnaw on. Traditionally, I would feed Benny healthier meals, but once in a blue moon, I would treat him to a few special extras to his kibble. I believed it's all about providing a balanced diet with the occasional treat for your pet, and I do my best to make sure he's getting the proper nutrition. It seems to have worked so far, as I've had Benny for seven years now, and he's been one of the best companions I've ever had.

After we ate and I took Benny for another walk, Phil and I decided to do one last round of writing before we began to pack things up for our eventual return to Toronto, and the hectic lives that awaited us upon our arrival. As much as we both dreaded the fact we would be getting back to reality, we both enjoyed the shared camaraderie over the past few days: the writing, the comfort food, the walks near the lake in the Kawarthas, and the bonding between two friends. It made me worry about when I dropped off

111

my writing compatriot back at his apartment. I was concerned Jessica was still staking out his building; however, if she really wanted to bust his ass, she would have made the trek up here and hauled him in. That being said, I was surprised she didn't make more of an effort to track me down. Then, I remembered that I did not have my phone turned on since Phil switched it off for me on the way up. I made a note to turn it back on during the drive back. I figured my voicemail must have been overflowing with messages from her.

"What time does the Overnight writing session start again?" I asked my friend, as we finished up our creative binge.

"It's going to start later this year because there's another event in the same venue just prior to it starting. We don't take over the place until 10:30 p.m."

"So, we'll hit the road about 7:30 or 8, then?"

Phil gave a thumbs up. "That sounds good. I'll help you close up the place."

"That would be greatly appreciated. It will cut down on the time it'll take."

I would take Benny for one final walk before we started to pack things up, and I closed down the cottage for the remainder of the winter. We gathered our belongings and loaded them into my car. By the time we pulled out of the driveway it was a little after 7:30 p.m., and we began the long drive back to the big city. I was concerned the traffic would be insane because of it being Championship Weekend, but I was fortunate that most of the crowds were centralized in the area between Dundas and Queen's Quay. Where I was dropping Phil off was just south of Bloor; well north of where all the action was.

~ * * * ~

I pulled into a service station in Bowmanville to top up my gas tank for the rest of our trip back to Toronto, and decided to turn on my cell phone. Sure enough, my mailbox was full with voicemail messages; the majority of which, I presumed, were from Jessica. I was about to punch into my archive when my phone rang with a new call. It turned out to be my partner.

"Celdom," I answered.

"Where the fuck have you been? I've been trying to get a hold of you for the past three days."

"I missed you too, Amerson," my voice dripping with sarcasm.

"Can it, Celdom. What the hell is going on?"

"Well, since I was thrown off the case, I decided to go off the grid for a few days. So, I gathered up Benny and headed up to my cottage."

"Your cottage? I thought you closed that up for the winter on Thanksgiving weekend."

"I did, but I bought a portable generator, and camped out there until tonight. I'm actually on my way back to Toronto right now. Have there been any new developments in the investigation?"

"There have been plenty of them. First off, that pattern Bennett picked up on for us was correct: two more homicides on Thursday, another two yesterday, and one final one earlier today."

"That makes it the fifteen he predicted would happen. Have you been able to track Bennett down?"

Jessica confessed, "Well, here's the thing. Bennett is not the killer. It was someone else."

I breathed a sigh of relief, but had to choose my words, as not to tip her off about Phil being with me. "See, I told you it wasn't him. So, who's the lowlife responsible for all of the carnage?"

"His name is Samuel Stevens. He's been a very vocal activist on the Canadian football message boards the past few months; bashing the Canadian game and promoting the American version in quite a spirited fashion. He hails from Niagara Region, but apparently has been renting out a motel room on Kingston Road for a week and a half now."

"Not far from Bennett's neck of the woods; thus, increasing the suspicion of our now innocent friend."

"It does appear that way. However, we're afraid he might strike again."

"Of course, the Boatmen have a shot at a sixteenth Championship title tomorrow night; which means, the potential for a sixteenth victim."

"That's my concern exactly. How far are you from Toronto right now?"

"I'm currently gassing up in Bowmanville. I'm dropping off some cargo before heading home."

Jessica was confused, "'Dropping off some cargo?'" Then, it dawned on her. "Bennett has been with you the whole time, hasn't he?"

"Sorry, Amerson, I still believed he didn't do it, and I didn't want you to lock up an innocent man."

"Goddamn it, Celdom! You do realize you were running the risk of harbouring a fugitive, right?"

"I will admit it was a gamble, but fortunately, he's been cleared of any wrongdoing, and it's saved you some unnecessary paperwork."

Jessica sighed, "Yeah, whatever. So, do you want to meet up, so we can go over the case so far?"

"Sure, meet me at my place in a couple of hours, and we can plot our attack from there."

"Great, I'll see you then."

"See you then, Amerson." I hung up my phone.

Finally, I was able to catch a break on this case. My hunch all along that my best friend was innocent came true. What's more, we had gotten a positive ID on the real culprit. I finished filling up my tank, and climbed back into my car. I had noticed Phil, who had been sleeping since we pulled onto the 401 in Port Hope, had woken up from his nap.

"Well, you seem to be in a chipper mood," he observed.

"I am, I just got off the phone with Jessica."

"You're upbeat from that? I would have thought she'd chew you out for not having your phone turned on for the past few days."

"She did, but she just informed me that we have an ID on our suspect."

"Oh, she did now, eh? Are there any specifics on the identity of this guy?"

"Apparently, he's an American football fan from the Niagara Region, who has been in town since the day before the first homicides up at the university a week and a half ago. He had been posting anti-Canadian football messages on a message board beforehand."

"And now, he's resorting to actual violence to get his message out even further."

"It appears that way. Jessica seems to think there might be a sixteenth murder tomorrow."

"Tomorrow's the actual Championship game. If your assailant is going to strike, it'll be either at the domed stadium, or at the tailgate party on Front Street before the game."

"Holy crap! If he's going to attack either of those venues, there's the potential for there to be more than one person killed."

"And hell knows how many more wounded in the hail of bullets. There is a good chance it could turn into a November version of the incident on Danzig."

"A tragedy the city has never fully recovered from, even though it happened all the way out in West Hill."

"If you and Jessica are going to have any shot at nipping this in the bud, you're going to have to have officers stationed everywhere from University over to Spadina between King and Lakeshore. It'll be a wide swath, but it'll probably be the best way to contain him."

"That's something I'll have to discuss with my partner when I meet her back at my place after dropping you off. Jessica will be the one that will have to rally the troops since I'm still off the clock officially until the first week of December."

"Well, hopefully the two of you will be able to devise a plan where you will be able to assist in an unofficial capacity."

The writer and I engaged in some more small talk, as we made our way back into the city. After pulling off the Don Valley Parkway onto Bloor, it was only a few more minutes until we pulled up to the Overnight writing session venue at Yonge and Charles. I felt a little unnerved being back at the building, as it was the site of the climax of the novel writing mass murder case from three years before. However, there was one good thing that came out of it: it was during the case where I would meet and befriend Phil, and that was something I will never regret doing. He gathered his things from my trunk, and we said our goodbyes. The writer thanked me again for the time away, and he said he 'owed' me. I didn't know how he would, but if I knew Phil, he would find a way to do so. After I saw that he gained safe entrance to the venue, I pulled away, and made my way home for my meeting with my partner.

CHAPTER 17

Fifteen minutes later, I pulled up to my little bungalow in the area of Pape and Cosburn to find Jessica waiting for me in her car. I honked my horn to let her know that I had arrived.

"Well now, look who finally decided to reveal himself," my partner quipped. "It's about time you got home."

I kissed my girlfriend, "A thousand pardons, dear, but it takes a good couple of hours to drive from my cottage to here. Plus, don't forget, I had to drop Phil off at the Overnight writing session for his novel writing thing down at Yonge and Charles first."

"He's seriously going to write all night long?"

"He certainly is. He'll be in there with others from 10:30 tonight until 8 o'clock tomorrow morning; writing for a good chunk of the time. They'll take breaks at various points to socialize, snack, and use the facilities."

"What do you mean 'snack'? Most places are closed at that hour, aren't they?"

"Most people will bring junk food and tea to share with everybody, like a pot-luck. But, should they crave something a little more substantial, there is a fast food restaurant on the corner, and just north of Bloor there is a 24-hour coffee shop. These people have been known to do a coffee run as a group up there at 4 o'clock in the morning."

Jessica shook her head in disbelief. "That is completely insane. I'm surprised you didn't join them tonight."

"As much as I'd like to, I don't think I could ever participate in another Overnight writing session; at least, not at that venue. That's where I had the final showdown during that mass murder case involving members of the Toronto Chapter of the novel writing challenge community. It still brings back a lot of bad memories."

Jessica caressed my face to comfort me. "I understand, but first and foremost, let's get all of your stuff unpacked."

"Thanks, Jessica. That would be greatly appreciated."

~ * * * ~

After helping bring the contents of what remained in the trunk of my car into my home, we decided to get down to brass tacks. I ended up brewing a pot of coffee for the two of us since I had a feeling it was going to be a long review session. In the back of my mind, I thought steeping a pot of tea might have been better, but there was no guarantee that it would have provided enough stimulating caffeine to help us power through our planning session. Once the brown liquid had finished dripping, I poured us a couple of mugs, prepared them according to our respective preferences, and commenced working on my dining room table.

"So, you mentioned over the phone that Stevens killed five more people as predicted, correct?" I began.

"Yep, two people on Thursday for the 11th and 12th victims, then, another two more yesterday for numbers 13 and 14, then this afternoon, the 15th body was reported."

"Have they been able to announce any specifics on the latest unfortunate five? You know, where the bodies were found, if they were Boatmen fans, or supporters for other teams; that sort of information?"

"It was a fairly even split between male and female victims for these five."

"Lay it on me, then."

"Well, in the Thursday incident, two females were killed by fatal gunshot wounds. They were a couple of local girls: a Victoria Tabor, aged 28, from Thornhill; the other was 25-year old Christine Secord of North York. Both of them were gunned down near Yonge-Dundas Square."

"Oh, lovely. That's not far from where one of the local TV stations is based. That will add fuel to the media firestorm."

"It gets worse from there. On Friday, two males tasted the hot lead served up by Stevens; both of them fans visiting from Calgary."

"A pair of Albertans. I guess Stevens wanted to diversify with a couple of supporters from the opposing side."

"Gary, this is a pro-American with hatred towards the Canadian game. In his eyes, everyone celebrating the Championship in town this week is 'from the opposing side.'"

"Duly noted. What are the particulars of the Cowtown corpses?"

"32-year old Dwight Somerset, and 36-year old Gordon Sarcee. They were on their way to Nathan Phillips Square for some free pancakes the Calgary hospitality committee were serving up."

"Wait, I thought that wasn't happening until today."

"Actually, they did a second session on Friday during the lunch hour. Now, I don't know if the bonus one was because Calgary is playing Sunday night, but it was a decent gesture on their part."

"It sounds like it was. It's just a shame that event was marred by Stevens' foul play."

"Yes, but his most recent victim was the most brazen of them all."

I took a sip from my mug of coffee. "What happened? Did Stevens open fire at one of the concerts being held as part of the Championship Week festivities?"

"Oh, this was much worse than that. Stevens snuck past security, entered one of the rooms at the hotel that's connected to the domed stadium, and garroted one of the halftime performers for the Championship game."

I was confused, "Garroted? You mean...?"

"Yep, Stevens wrapped some fishing line around the victim's throat and choked them to death."

"That is horrific." I said. "However, it could be very significant if Stevens not only didn't want to be heard, but wanted his victim to die quietly, too."

"Considering who the 15th death was," Jessica stated, "I'm sure there are a lot of people who wished he wasn't heard at all."

When my partner said that, I envisioned hearing the millions of young girls around the world screaming in sorrow. For his 15th sacrifice, Samuel Stevens killed the Canadian singing sensation, Jesse Billings. This would come as a newsflash with reactions from both sides of the spectrum. To his legion of fans, they had just lost their idol, their 'raison d'être.' For the hard-core Canadian football fans that would be tuning into – or attending – the big game, it was a relief to their ears, as they believed the teen heartthrob from southwestern Ontario had no business being in the same spotlight as the national celebration of the sport. Stevens saved his biggest slaying for last, or did he? There was still the concern we both had that he would strike once more before the game; thus, possibly adding a sixteenth body to his resume. It was then I decided to strategize with my girlfriend-in-arms.

"As noteworthy and tragic as the Billings murder is," I mentioned, "we have to prepare for the possibility of one more attack by Stevens."

"That is my concern, too. Where do you think he may strike?"

"Well, according to Bennett, the most likely venues would be at the stadium itself or on Front Street during the outdoor tailgate party."

"Those seem to be the most logical places. How are we going to plan this counterstrike?"

Jessica and I spent the next couple of hours formulating our plan. As suggested by Phil, we would have officers stationed at various checkpoints along the perimeter of the tailgate and stadium zone; bordered by Spadina to the west, King to the north, University to the east, and Lakeshore

Boulevard to the south. The reinforcements would be set up at the main intersections along those boundaries. What's more, Jessica and I would be patrolling the tailgate party in case Stevens made an appearance. If our hunch was correct, he would be showing up at some point.

By the time we had everything planned out, and told the Division our staffing requirements, it was well after 1 o'clock in the morning. Jessica and I would be starting our foot patrol in another 12 hours. A look outside my window showed a few light flurries falling from the sky. It wasn't anything substantial, but enough to provide a very thin layer of white on our vehicles.

"This is going to make for some slippery driving conditions heading back to Cabbagetown," my partner noted.

"It will probably melt away by the afternoon."

"That is most likely. I guess I should start heading home."

"You know, if you're not willing to risk it, you're more than welcome to spend the night."

Jessica smirked, "I'm not going to sleep in the same bed as you, Gary."

"I didn't say we had to. You could sleep in my bed, while I crash out on the couch."

"Uh huh, until you got up to use the bathroom; then, in your half-asleep stupor, you head into your room, and climb into bed with me. That's not happening yet, buddy."

"I promise I wouldn't do that," I attempted to reassure. However, it would be all for naught, as Jessica kissed my cheek, told me she would see me in the morning, and pulled away from my house in her car.

I doubted I would have put the moves on my girlfriend considering the hour; I was just trying to be hospitable, but I understood that she wasn't ready to take that step yet. One of the biggest knocks on me was my quickness to end up in bed with a woman I really like. It happened with

Karen, and it happened when I was with Elaine. I was trying to change my ways with Jessica, but it appeared my former fiancée warned my current love interest about my past, and it had made her cautious about how far we do end up going in our relationship. We do love and care for each other, there is no mistaking that. However, since the two of us work side-by-side, it makes for a different dynamic to our relationship. Regardless, I was very fortunate to have Jessica Amerson in my life, and right now, I didn't want there to be any complications between her and I.

I stood on my stoop for a few seconds more, as I saw the minute flakes of snow descend from the night sky – enjoying the first signs of winter's evidential arrival – before I returned inside and commenced getting ready for bed. Tomorrow was Samuel Stevens' day of reckoning.

CHAPTER 18

I woke up on Sunday morning with a sudden burst of energy; which was odd given the early hour I had risen. Normally, I liked to sleep in on my Sundays off, and given the fact I was in the midst of yet another two week suspension, today was an ample opportunity to do so. However, I had to rise and shine at the crack of the late November dawn, as I was about to do some undercover work with Jessica in a bid to put an end to the reign of terror caused by one Samuel Stevens over the previous ten days.

It was the belief of not only my partner and I, but our trusted civilian friend, Phil Bennett, that Stevens would be making an appearance at the Outdoor Tailgate Party outside of the Canadian professional football Championship game, and possibly unleashing a hail of bullets in a bid to add a sixteenth – if not more – body to the death toll he had amassed over the past week and a half. There would be thousands of people flocking to Front Street for the event before they filed into the domed stadium for the big game between Calgary and the hometown Boatmen; all of them ripe to be picked off should Stevens have the sadistic inkling to do so. It was something both Jessica and I wanted to curtail, if possible. Thankfully, we had additional officers stationed in the area around not only the outdoor festivities, but the stadium, as well; in the event Stevens decided to delay his attempt until he got to the Championship game's venue instead. However, I had a sinking feeling he might attempt to infiltrate the proceedings undetected, but I didn't know how. It was something that unnerved me, but at the same time, helped drive me to get him behind bars once and for all.

After going through my usual morning routine, I hopped into my car, and drove to a public lot near the Division. I would have been reprimanded had I driven into the police lot, but since Jessica needed me alongside of her, I had to meet up with her under cloak and dagger. I waited for her to pull out of the garage while sipping on a store-bought coffee; biding my time and thinking about the fact our mission would be akin to trying to find a needle in a haystack. Regardless, I was confident that Stevens would be found out by my partner, yours truly, or one of the officers on the perimeter. I just wished they would have mobilized soon, as the chilled winds were starting to howl.

Five minutes later, I heard a car horn being honked. I looked over and saw Jessica acknowledging my presence. I hurried over to her vehicle and climbed in.

"It took you long enough, Amerson," I complained.

"Sorry it took so long, Celdom. Lt. Davies' morning briefing went a little longer than normal."

"I guess because of all the officers being on-call to secure the area."

"Have you been waiting long?"

"Probably ten... fifteen minutes, tops."

"And yet, you didn't buy me a coffee. Some partner you are."

"I would have, but remember, they're not supposed to know that I'm with you on this potential bust. I'm supposed to be at home, cooling my heels."

"Yes, I know, but still, some coffee that's better than the swill they serve in the Break Room would be nice."

"I'll make it up to you on the way back to the Division."

"Considering I'm letting you tag along, you better make it a large. You owe me big time."

I chuckled at my partner, and even did a "Yes, Mistress. Anything you say, Mistress," like a henchman in one of those old black-and-white monster movies. Jessica punched my arm in jest, but she was thankful I was there to help her out. As much as she hated my jokes from time-to-time, the two of us did have a good chemistry together. It's what helped us be an effective team, and in turn, a good couple when we were off-duty. I hoped she wouldn't get into trouble with our superiors if it was learned that she had me come along with her on this mission. However, since I was working pro-bono, there shouldn't have been too much of a stink caused. It's not like I was carrying my badge or gun with me; I had to turn those in earlier on in the week when Lt. Davies told me to bugger off for a fortnight. I just wished I had more of an official capacity today, but such was the case.

The two of us pulled into an underground parking garage at the foot of University and made our way into the heart of the festivities; all the while, we kept our eyes peeled for any sign of Samuel Stevens. It was just before noon – the game would not start for another six hours – yet, there were fans milling about; taking in the atmosphere. I noticed fans from across the country had made their way to Toronto for the big game; however, with Toronto playing in the Championship game, the majority of the attendees were wearing the familiar colour combination of Cambridge Blue and Oxford Blue in support of their hometown team. I scanned the crowd to see if Phil had actually made the trek in from Scarborough for the soiree, but then I remembered that he was up all night writing up at Yonge and Charles. If he did show up he would have been dead on his feet. I'll admit he's a crazy son of a bitch, but I don't think he would have forgone sleep to have gone into a potentially dangerous situation. I'd like to think he valued his safety over hanging out with a bunch of fellow football fans.

As I was surveying the area, I was also keeping my ears open for any clues as to when and where Stevens might gain entry. It wasn't until I overheard two fans talking that I received a vital piece of information.

"There doesn't seem to be a lot of people here," a male dressed in the Green and White colours of the team from Regina bemoaned.

"It's still early yet," his friend, another male, donned in Green and Gold garb of the squad from Edmonton replied. "Besides, the Fan Parade hasn't started yet."

Yours truly, being the curious individual that I was, interjected into the conversation. "Excuse me," I interrupted, "what is this Fan Parade you're talking about?"

The Edmonton supporter explained, "There is a big fan rally and Parade that's starting up at the stadium by the university on... Bloor Street, I think it is... and making its way down to the Tailgate Party."

"Is that the one where they're marching with the Championship trophy?" the Regina fan queried.

"Yep. It's a new event that they're doing this year. There's going to be fans from every team taking part; all wearing their teams' colours and waving their flags."

"That will be interesting to see," I acknowledged. "Thanks for explaining it."

"No problem," they smiled.

I excused myself from the conversation, and made my way back to my partner to tell her what I had learned.

"So, what's the word?" she enquired.

"Apparently, there is a Fan Parade going on where they're marching with the Championship Trophy from the downtown university stadium down to here. If my hunch is correct, Stevens will try to infiltrate the party with that band, in a bid to be inconspicuous, and then plan his attack from there."

"From the university, you say? Depending on the route the marchers will take, they might not be here for a couple of hours."

"Especially, if they decide to pass by the two 'fan zones' at Yonge and Dundas, and Nathan Phillips Square en route. There's a possibility Stevens could integrate with the throng as they progress through downtown."

"That's a possibility, but could be concerning, as well."

"How do you figure?"

"Think about it, Celdom. If Canadian football fans are on his hit list..."

Then, it dawned on me, "Oh my God, they would all be sitting ducks."

"It is something to worry about, but it would probably seem too easy for Stevens. There wouldn't be much of a cover for him to make his escape. Waiting until he's down here to unleash his fury would be easier for him to move in, execute his damage, and make a quick get-away."

"So, if the Parade is proceeding directly here from City Hall, we should put the security detail along University, as well as, at King and Simcoe on alert."

"I'm on it." Jessica got on her wireless to let the reinforcements know.

It was a good thing my partner invited me along, so I could be an extra set of eyes and ears on the mission. If it wasn't for me, we wouldn't know of this likely method for the sick psychopath to gain entry into the area. The Parade would provide a perfect cover for him. However, I came to the realization that a guy wearing an American football jacket in an entourage of Canadian football fan would make him stick out like a sore thumb. Stevens would have to change his garb in order to look more inconspicuous. I was at a loss at how he might be able to pull this off, but then it came to me: 'the U.S. Experiment.'

Phil had told me about what happened in the mid 1990's when the Canadian professional league tried their hand at expanding into the United States. While it seemed like a novel idea, the plan faltered because the bulk of the franchises were in southern markets. The experiment would have been more of a success if the teams were situated closer to the Canadian border, but regardless, they still attempted to pull it off over the three years that it lasted. In all, seven American cities would host Canadian football games at some point during the era before the league scrapped the concept. If I knew Stevens, he would most likely don a jersey from one of those seven different clubs, or would he?

I faintly remembered a couple of teams on this side of the border that had come and gone over the years; Ottawa being a prime example. Stevens could also possibly sport the black, white, and red from one of the two clubs that used to call the Nation's Capital home. There were many disguise options he had, but until we saw him for certain, Jessica and I were in the dark as much as everyone else. All we could do was stand on alert, and wait.

After 90 minutes, I was beginning to think that Stevens was on to us, and wasn't going to show until Jessica's wireless squelched. It was the officers manning the King and Simcoe checkpoint. The marchers in the Fan Parade were approaching their spot, and they would keep us informed if they spotted the maniac that had been causing havoc on our streets over the recent days. Jessica turned to me, and told me to get ready for the infusion of more fans, and the possibility the lowlife we had been looking for might be amongst them. I could feel my heart pumping my body full of adrenaline; it was a feeling I always experienced whenever I was about to confront a suspect one-on-one for the penultimate time. I felt it when I went toe-to-toe with the man who murdered my former partner, Rob McManus, after he had kidnapped my former Barbadian girlfriend, and held her hostage. But, that was just one of the times I had 'gotten in the zone.' I was ready for Stevens, and whatever he was going to throw at my partner and me.

Five minutes later, Jessica's wireless went off again.

"Amerson," an officer, Constable Slater, reported, "we've spotted Stevens. He's amongst the marchers; wearing a Baltimore jersey. Stevens is heading your way as we speak."

"Thanks, Slater. I'm on it." Jessica turned to me. "Celdom, its 'go time.'"

I nodded at my partner, and we wove our way through the crowd in our quest to find our culprit. Suddenly, I saw the man we had been on the trail of for the past ten days walking down Simcoe; crossing Wellington. He was a 6-foot tall stocky-built Caucasian male, wearing a dark blue replica jersey that was worn by the Baltimore franchise that hoisted the Championship in Regina back in 1995. Adorned on top of his head was a ball cap; showcasing the logo of the franchise that once played in the Maryland metropolis over a decade ago.

"Samuel Stevens," I called out to him. "Could we have a word with you, please?"

He must have noticed Jessica reaching for her badge because the next thing I saw was him reaching into the side of his jeans and pulled out a 9-millimetre caliber handgun.

"Everybody, get down now!" my partner exclaimed, as Stevens fired a shot in our direction. The crowd of fans in the immediate area scurried out of harm's way. Jessica fired a retaliatory shot, and the chase was on. We trailed him down Wellington over to John, then south on John to Front, and then cut across the front of the Convention Centre, as there was a hail of bullets being exchanged. Every time we saw an opening, Jessica fired off a couple of shots in an attempt to hit the assailant in his arm, but then Stevens would unload a couple of shots in return; forcing us to duck for cover. We tracked him over to the corner of Front and Simcoe, where he turned south again.

"He's heading towards Skywalk," I observed.

"If he makes it there, he's got a clear run all the way back to Union Station. We can't let him get in the walkway."

We hurried over to the intersection, and stood behind the corner of the hotel that's situated on the southwest corner. Jessica reloaded her pistol, and was about to fire a couple more bullets in his direction. Then, all of a sudden, Stevens fired a shot, but it didn't appear to go anywhere near my partner and I. The two of us looked at each other to see if either of us, or any part of our cover, had been struck by the bullet, but there was no real damage to any of it. The two of us cautiously approached the corner of Simcoe and Station, and noticed Stevens was laid out and bleeding from his forehead. However, kneeling above the now out cold assailant and restraining him was a vigilant Bennett.

"That was for all of the deaths you've caused before you killed off that annoying Jesse Billings," the writer uttered, breathing heavily.

I put my gun back into my holster. "Bennett," I said, "you caught Stevens, but how?"

"I was coming out of Union Station and heading towards the Street Party, when I heard shots ring out. Knowing what I did of the case you guys were working on, I ducked for cover, and precariously made my way down Station. That was when I saw your shooter hiding behind the corner of the building here. I figured he was firing at either the crowds or the police, so I tackled him from behind; driving his face into the corner of the building, then smashing it into the sidewalk."

"But what about that last shot he fired?

"His gun went off as I was forcing him to the ground. The bullet struck the asphalt and ricocheted into the side of the hotel across the street; just missing the entrance to its underground garage. I just hope this will shut your girlfriend up about me being the guy responsible for all of this Championship-related bloodshed."

Jessica's jaw dropped. "You heard about that? How did you know?"

"When Detective Celdom stopped for gas in Bowmanville our way back to Toronto last night, I heard the two of you talking on his cell phone. Look, I don't blame you guys for thinking as such; you were just doing your job. But, the least you two could have done was to have been up front with me, and let me know that I was under investigation."

"I know, and I apologize for that. I just want to thank you for helping us catch Stevens before he added another body to the already hefty death count."

Phil chuffed, "Yeah, whatever."

"What's wrong?" I asked.

He looked at me and sighed, "Look, Detective Celdom, I'm glad to have helped you catch the guy responsible for all of the carnage the past few days, but to have my own friend and his partner-slash-girlfriend accuse me of such heinous crimes that I did not commit... well, it hurts and offends me greatly. After all of this, it's made me consider Amy's offer."

Jessica was surprised, "Amy? Are you two back together?"

"We are, but she's also asked me to move in with her. And, given recent events, it makes me think it's time to move on from Toronto, and relocate indefinitely to the Forest City."

My partner and I didn't say a word as he said, "Goodbye, Detectives." Phil walked up the stairs to Skywalk, and returned to Union Station via the covered walkway. We stood there in shocked silence, as the realization that this investigation had cost me my best friend washed over me.

CHAPTER 19

It was very rare when I found myself at a loss for words during my 27-year career with the Toronto P.D. When a partner of mine couldn't think of a thing to say to me, either, was even less likely. Yet, as the two of us drove back to the Division, Jessica and I still could not fully allow ourselves to let the recent revelation to sink in. My best friend – the one guy I had been able to bond with that wasn't a work colleague – was leaving my life because of all the events over the past week and a half. What's more, he cited it was the fact we had listed him as a suspect in the brutal murders of 15 people; even though, I initially believed he was innocent. Because it was my girlfriend who planted that seed of doubt in my mind, I felt angry at her; however, I did realize she was just doing her job, as I was trying to do, too, in the end. I wanted to tear a strip off of her, but didn't feel it was right to lash out. The nervous look on her face made me think she thought I was going to; that was why she didn't say anything for the entire drive. However, once we pulled into the garage at the Division, and parked our car, we felt the tense feelings needed to be cut.

"Well," Jessica sighed, "that was a rather uncomfortable return to the office."

I made a sarcastic comment, "If that was your attempt to ease the tension of the situation, then you've failed miserably."

"Gary, please. I know you're upset right now."

"Thank you, Miss Obvious."

"You don't have to be an asshole about it," Jessica shot back.

"Well, excuse me! How else do you think I'm supposed to feel right now? I just lost my best friend in the line of duty. But no, he wasn't shot. I got talked into thinking he was a cold blooded killer by my colleague. I never should have listened to you in the first place."

"Damn it, Celdom! How many times do I have to apologize? We're officers of the law, and we were doing our job. Did I err in my judgment? Absolutely, but I'm going to be damned if I'm going to let you hang it over my head for the rest of my life!"

My partner was about to storm out of the vehicle when her door suddenly slammed shut, and locked itself. It was then, a familiar voice of reason decided to make her presence felt.

"I see I'm going to have to be the one to smooth things over between you two again," Karen commented from the backseat.

"Now, see what you've done?" I accused Jessica.

"Oh, quit being a dick, Gary."

"At least I'm not a sanctimonious bitch who turned me against my best bud."

"Good God," Karen screamed, "will you two please shut the fuck up!"

Jessica and I stared at each other with daggers in each other's eyes, but decided to give the spectre the opportunity to let her opinion be heard.

"Now, Gary, you have to realize that Jessica was only doing what she thought was the right thing to do: identify and capture the individual responsible for the bloodbath that had transpired over the past fortnight. Granted, she named the wrong person initially, and the real killer eventually revealed himself, but she was doing her job as an officer of the law, and you can't slight her for that."

"I know I shouldn't," I resigned. "It's just that I knew in my heart that Bennett wasn't the guy who had pulled the trigger all of those times. Does he have his share of issues? Absolutely, what with the gambling problem and his mental health concerns over the years. Shit, I wouldn't be surprised if with all of this stress Jessica and I have put him through, he ended up having another relapse."

"I hope he doesn't resort to that," Jessica worried.

"Jessica, please," the spectre halted.

I continued, "But, I still didn't want to believe all of the evidence that had accumulated to the point where he was considered a prime suspect. I mean, the fact all of the murders occurred in locations where Bennett was in relative close proximity to. It's almost as if Stevens wanted to frame my friend; just because Phil was noted as being a Ti-Cat fan living in Toronto."

Karen said, "It did appear that way. However, take into consideration the one key factoid that disproved those earlier accusations."

"That being?"

"When you and Jessica first interviewed Phil all those days ago in the coffee shop by his place, he had a hunch back then that it was a pro-American football fan – in this case, Samuel Stevens -- who wanted to make a statement where the Boatmen should pack up shop so the mighty league from the south could establish a permanent franchise here. Stevens believed that by doing so during the Canadian Football Championship Week would give all the media attention his plight could get to his cause."

"Not to mention the ominous number of murders he committed," Jessica added.

"Right," I acknowledged. "The number of people killed was equal to the number of titles the Boatmen have won over the Championship's existence. That was a bit of symbolism Phil was able to pick up on."

"It's a good thing he has been a fan of the game for so long that he was able to notice such a pattern."

"That's what comes from following the Canadian game for over 30 years. Sure, he may cheer for a rival club, but Bennett is a guy who is a fan of the sport and its history. Granted, he wasn't too thrilled with the 'American expansion' experiment back in the mid-90s, but he grit his teeth and beared it; especially when Baltimore beat Calgary in the Championship back in

'95 – the only time the title had ever been awarded to an American club in the game's now 100 editions."

Karen was quick to bring the conversation back to the initial bone of contention, "But, despite all of that, you cannot fault your partner for doing her job."

"Thank you," Jessica complimented.

My former fiancée turned her attention to my girlfriend, "However, it should also be noted that you did not really investigate all the possible avenues. You were quick to finger Bennett based on those preconceived notions you formulated initially. A proper detective would have done more thorough investigating in finding the real culprit, instead of going on that first hunch."

"I just assumed that..."

"Assumed? Assumed?!? You know the story of what happens when you assume."

Jessica rolled her eyes. "I know, I know. 'You make an ass out of you and me.' Personally, I think that is a rather lame expression, but that's just my opinion."

"Be it as it may, you did not perform due diligence. Because of that, the man who you said yourself was 'the best friend Gary had outside of the Division' is now looking at moving out of his life."

"I could understand Bennett would be upset and offended over my countless accusations, but I didn't think he would actually consider pulling up stakes and leave the city he's called home for the past 35 years."

"Well, he was hurt and took umbrage to it. Now, thanks to all of the mess you two have caused, he's now exploring this option which has been offered to him. I'm not sure you truly realize that."

My girlfriend sat in the passenger's seat and let what Karen said sink in. She had experienced hurt feelings before, and stormed off in a huff before.

Most notably was a mere couple of months ago when Jessica learned of how 'serious' things were initially between myself and Elaine in the final days of my investigation down in Barbados into the death of my former colleague, Rob McManus. My girlfriend had dumped a bowl of salad over my head, and marched out of my house in an upset rage. It was Karen who provided a voice of reason, and helped patch things up between the two of us. We were still trying to smooth things over, and it was a concern that the events of this case might have been a setback in our repairs. Now, Jessica was starting to see the error of her ways, and a feeling of remorse began to wash over her.

"I'm sorry, Gary," my partner apologized. "I really should have explored all of the angles instead of focusing on one particular suspect. I have no one to blame, but myself. Can you ever forgive me?"

Jessica looked at me with a hopeful look in her eyes, but I was reluctant to turn my gaze towards her. It wasn't until Karen smacked me on the back of my head that I was able to force myself to look at my girlfriend. At first, I was still steaming, but once I looked into her eyes, my foul demeanor began to melt away.

"Oh, how could I stay mad at that face?" I caved. "Of course, I forgive you, Jessica."

"Thank you, sweetheart." We shared a sweet kiss.

Karen smiled, "There you go. Now, since you two have patched things up, we can get back to normal."

I thought out loud, "I just wish there was some way we can talk to Phil, so we can try to convince him that our antics are not just cause for him to pull up stakes and move two hours away."

Jessica sighed, "I wish there was, too."

"Actually," Karen pointed out, "you guys might have a shot in talking him out of it."

I was confused. "What do you mean?"

"Didn't the two of you notice the lack of conviction in his voice when he announced his decision? He sounded like he was not really ready to make that type of commitment."

"Are you saying what I think you're saying?" Jessica asked.

"If you're thinking that you might have a shot to get him to change his mind, then you are right on the money."

"Are you positive of that?" I asked. I don't want us to make the trip all the way to Scarborough to find out that our efforts are all for naught."

"To be honest, I think if the two of you show up together, that might solidify his resolve and you'll lose him forever. If only one of you go, you might be able to sell him on the benefits of staying here in Toronto."

I turned to my girlfriend, and shared a silent look to see who should be the person to talk to Phil. If Jessica made the trip to his home, then it might be a tougher pitch since she was the one who initially suggested he was a suspect. Bennett might turn on her, and he would be on the first bus to the Forest City. However, if I was the one to speak on behalf of the two of us, I might have a better chance in getting him to remain.

Jessica suggested, "Gary, perhaps you should be the one to speak to him."

"I was thinking the same thing. Since I've known Bennett longer, I might be able to sway his opinion in getting him to stay."

"I concur," Karen chimed in. "It's probably for the best that Gary to be the one to have a heart-to-heart with the writer. Besides, after all of this crap, his novel writing attempt might have gone down the toilet. As someone who participates in the monthly challenge, as well, Gary might be able to empathise with Bennett and give him some words of encouragement to get him over this final hump; in the event he has fallen behind in this year's attempt."

Jessica nodded. "That's a very valid point. Go, Gary. If you hurry, you might be able to bring him a peace offering of coffee and donuts from the store near his place before it closes when you make your pitch."

I checked my watch, and saw that if I was able to take advantage of her suggestion, I would need to get the lead out and boot it to the Markham Road and Eglinton area before it got too late. I knew he was still currently living with his roommate of the past 5 years for the time being. But, unless I was persuasive enough, he would be living in different city 130 miles due west. My latest moment of reckoning was nigh, and it was time for me to spring into action.

I leaned over, kissed Jessica once again, climbed out of the police-issued vehicle, and headed over to my personal set of wheels. "I'm going to head out there now," I replied. "Wish me luck, you two. I just hope this works."

"I hope so, too, Celdom," Jessica worried. "Best of luck."

Karen gave a ghostly pat on Jessica's back, and suggested, "I'll go with him for additional support. Should he start to falter, I'll be there to help get him back on track."

"That would be greatly appreciated."

Karen and I climbed into my vehicle, and prepared for the long drive to the eastern reaches of the city; all the while, rehearsing my sales pitch. I didn't know how successful I was going to be – mostly because I had never been much of a salesman – however, if I was going to keep my best friend in my life, this was the only shot I was going to get, so I had better be damn convincing.

CHAPTER 20

I pulled into the Visitor's parking lot adjacent to Phil's apartment building with a box of donut holes and a couple 14-ounce serving cups of coffee. I couldn't remember how my friend usually took his caffeinated beverage, so I ended up giving him the traditional way most Canadians have their java from the store: two shots of cream and two teaspoons of sugar. I made my way to the front door of the building with my cargo, but once I reached over to check the listing for what buzzer code to press, I was at for a loss. I could not find his name on the posted list. It dawned on me that the apartment was probably listed in his roommate's name, since he had already been living there when Phil moved in. I didn't want to give my friend a call on my cell phone since this was a surprise visit, so I was at a loss for what to do next. That was until I looked over and noticed the front door was slightly ajar. The hinge on the lock was slightly damaged; thus, allowing individuals some easy access to the building. I just shook my head at the shoddy maintenance of the building, but decided to take advantage of the opportunity handed to me. I entered the building's lobby, then pulled out my notebook, scribbled a note about the faulty lock hinge, slipped it into the main office's mail slot before I rang for an elevator to take me to the 12th floor of the structure.

During the short lift ride up, Karen and I went over my plan of attack. I was to discuss with Phil the real reasons behind his snap decision to pull up stakes and move away. He did mention that he had gotten back together with his former girlfriend from last year. Also, Bennett stated that she was the one who propositioned him into moving down to London. Was this something that appealed to him? Phil reported he had been a resident of this neighbourhood for 35 years. He had seen it change a lot in that time, and for all I knew, it probably was not for the better. However, I had to pick his brain to know for certain, and ease my psyche over the hanging notion that Jessica and I were the breaking point in his choice.

I got off the elevator, and proceeded to walk down the hall towards his apartment door. I had to resist the urge to gag as I passed by the adjacent garbage room en route. I opened the door to the little cubby room to find that one of the other residents had left a couple of plastic grocery bags on the floor, a third was sitting in the chute without it being shoved down. I carefully disposed of the refuse and chalked that up on another reason why my friend would want to leave the neighbourhood. After regaining my senses, I knocked on Phil's door and waited for someone to answer. The only problem was it wasn't my friend who opened the door.

Before me stood a tall male dressed in a blue bath robe and black pajama pants. "Can I help you?" he asked, slightly annoyed that someone would come calling at this hour.

"I'm sorry to disturb you. Is Phil Bennett home?"

"He's in his room. Who should I say is calling?"

I flashed my badge and ID. "Detective Gary Celdom, Toronto P.D. I'm a friend of Phil's."

"Phil," he called out in a jovial voice, "the police are here to take you away."

"This really isn't official police business. I just wanted to talk to him on a personal level, Mister...?"

"Marsden, Jim Marsden."

Phil came from the back of his apartment, wearing a pair of green pajama pants and a multi-coloured sweatshirt. His initial look was of slight annoyance. "What the fuck are you doing here, Detective Celdom?"

"I just wanted to talk to you for a bit, completely off the record since I'm off-duty."

"You can try your best, but my mind is pretty much made up. I see you've met my roommate."

"I have." I acknowledged the man now sitting in the recliner. Jim was probably only a few years older than Phil, but stood a couple inches shorter than my friend. You couldn't see it from head-on, but it looked like my friend's roommate was developing a slight bald spot on the back of his head. Then, I realized my peace offering. "I brought coffee and donuts from the shop on the corner. My apologies for not bringing any coffee for your roommate, I didn't think he would be home yet."

"It's alright, Detective. If I had any coffee now, I would be up all night, and I have to be into work early tomorrow."

Phil asked, "The mincemeat pie and stollen production is in full swing now, isn't it?"

"Right up until Christmas. Should I leave you two to talk alone?"

"If you wouldn't mind please?"

"Does Jim know about your decision?"

"I haven't told him yet. I was going to wait until the New Year to do so."

"Told me what? You're not falling off the wagon again, are you, Phil?"

"No, nothing like that."

"It's nothing gambling related, Jim, but you might find yourself alone in this apartment next year. Apparently, our writing friend here is taking his ball and going down to London to move in with Amy."

"Gary!"

Jim wanted us to back up. "Whoa, whoa, you mean to tell me that you're moving out? What the hell brought this on?"

"It's a long story."

"And one that's bound to give me some sleepless nights in the process, so please, fill me in on the details."

"I'll fill you in on some of the circumstances so far. Phil was wrongfully implicated in a string of homicides which had transpired in the city over the past couple of weeks; something that my partner regrets in presuming, when I felt he was innocent all along."

Phil fumed, "And I was, until you bought into what Detective Amerson was suggesting."

"I know, and I truly regret in doing so, but you have to understand where she was coming from."

The writer sighed, "I don't fault you, Gary, you two were just doing your jobs; I get that. But, it just hurt me that my own friend would think that I would actually murder someone. Granted, I do get upset and frustrated at times, and in that rage I may say things that I eventually regret later on, but despite all of my anger, I would never harm a living being intentionally."

"I know you wouldn't, and in hindsight, I should have done a more vigilant job in convincing my partner in the first place. But, regardless of that, is it really worth pulling up stakes, and moving to a city a good two hour drive away? What about all of your friends here?"

"Friends? As if! Aside from you, Detective Amerson, and Jim, and maybe Siobhan, I don't really have any friends here in Toronto."

"What about the writing compatriots in the novel writing campaign? Surely, there have to be some people amongst them that would miss you if you moved away."

Seriously, you think the writing compatriots would miss me? You have got to be fucking kidding me. Let me let you in on something, Gary. Do you know how much bonding I do with all of those writers outside of November?"

"Given the reaction you're giving me, I'm presuming not a whole lot."

"Try none. Now, I don't know if it's because I'm all the way out here in Scarborough, and all of them are practically west of Yonge Street, or the fact that my perception that certain members have formed a nice little clique. But, the fact of the matter is, it's a young group who apparently thinks they've never left high school. Then again, some of those smug individuals practically are. Personally, I wouldn't mind if it was an age discrimination thing, but when one of the 'in crowd' is a guy who is just a mere couple of months younger than yours truly, it makes me fucking sick."

"Well, let's be honest, Phil," Jim offered. "You're not really one of the more sociable people out there."

"What the fuck is that supposed to mean?"

"Just look at you. You spend all day at the computer, chatting up with Amy online, or hanging out in the novel writing chat room during the month. Yet, you don't actually venture out of the apartment for actual social interaction. I mean, sure, you go to your addiction counselling meetings every week, but aside from those, do you really hang out with any of the people in those groups?"

"Admittedly, I don't."

"And why exactly is that? It can't be because of that social phobia you have. If it were, you wouldn't even leave the apartment to attend those."

"As much as I hate to agree with your roommate," I chimed in," he does have a valid point. What about that volunteering gig you have down at the health club you were telling about last month. That should be some sort of social interaction for you."

"It is, but it's just not the same. I mean, I go there to help people out and all, but it's not like I go out with any of them for coffee or anything similar."

"Have you even taken any initiative to go and ask them out for a coffee?"

"Well, not really. I don't really feel comfortable in doing so."

"Phil," Jim commented, "I don't know why you have this poor self-image of yourself. You say that you're a shy person, but in all of the time I've known you, you've proven yourself anything but. You're the type of guy who would strike up random conversations with complete strangers just because you heard them discussing something that you want to add your two cents on."

"Jim does have a point there. I remember when we first met three years ago, you seemed rather shy at first, but once you started to feel comfortable with those around you, you began to open up. So, is it really a matter of not feeling comfortable with those around you? Or, is it something more deep rooted that is preventing you from making new friends?"

"I think it's something more complex than that."

"Something psychological, perhaps?"

"You could call it that. I don't know if it was because of the way I was raised, but I've never really been one to open myself up to others. Some people may argue that it was the fact that I felt I lead a secluded lifestyle in my younger years; a self-perception that I had an overbearing caregiver."

"You mean your grandmother?" Jim asked.

"Exactly. I grew up believing that because of the generation gap, or perhaps the fact I was raised in a non-traditional family grouping, that I would not be as welcome with others; plus, the fact I felt that my grandmother was somewhat overbearing in my older years. I mean, it was like anything I wanted to do I had to get prior clearance by her. Of course, I was never one for the bar and club scene to begin with, but all the same."

"But, you didn't have to go to those to have a good time either," I pointed out.

"I know that. I just preferred regular interactions at wherever I happened to be because I felt it was more convenient; whether it be at the fitness centre, at school, or even at a sporting event. However, I never really felt confident to venture beyond that comfort zone."

"I see." I scratched my chin. "Do you think there was an underlying reason for that?"

"In retrospect, I was trying to be mindful of my life at home. I'll admit I was not the most understanding waif in the later years; my grandmother and I would always clash about things I wanted to do. But, I guess deep down, I respected her, and I didn't want to upset her in the end. In essence, I was pretty much a 'Mama's boy.'"

"Or, grandmother's boy, in this instance," Jim quipped with a chuckle.

"Jim, please."

"No, it's alright. I offered that bit of information up, so I'm willing to leave myself open to ridicule."

"But, getting back to the matter at hand here, despite the fact that you are upset about this whole investigation, there has to be some other reason why you are considering moving away from this neighbourhood; the same one you've called home for the past three and a half decades."

"It's not because of me, is it? I know I may make the odd crack at you on occasion, but you do realize it's all in good fun."

"Relax, Jim, it's not that. You and I are still on good terms. It's just I personally feel the city has outgrown me. Things have changed so much over the years; some of which, not for the better. Case in point, you know that massive shooting here in Scarborough this past July?"

"You mean the gang-related one by Morningside and Lawrence where two people were killed and 23 others injured?" I questioned.

"That would be the one. You know that's just three miles east of here?"

"But, Phil, that area has been bad for years."

"Jim does bring up a valid point. The area is pretty close to where that big gang by Kingston and Galloway call home, and everyone knows they've been embroiled in a gang war with a rival faction up in northeastern Scarborough."

"Be it as it may, it's just another reason why I don't feel like staying here for much longer."

Jim attempted to make his case, "Listen, Phil, I know that Toronto does have its flaws with crime and all, but there are also a lot of advantages it has over a smaller city like London."

"Such as?"

"Well, just look at the differences in public transit. Here, you have the benefits of a thorough bus network that can get you practically anywhere in the city; plus, the added bonus of having a subway that can shuttle you from one end to the heart of downtown in less than 45 minutes. Does London have that?"

"Not really. They only have their own bus system, and admittedly, it's not as frequent as it is here in Toronto."

"And not only that, there are tons of things one can do here in the big city. You could go to a museum, take in a sporting event, or if you want to feel more culturally refined, go to the opera or symphony. What sorts of entertainment options are there where Amy lives?"

"Well, London has a couple of theatres where you can go see a stage production; like that community players' performance of that World War II play Amy and I attended last year. I believe there's an art gallery just off of downtown by the river, as well, but we've yet to check that out. So, there are options available. However, I do have to admit, getting to a movie theatre from her place down there takes longer than it would here. It's not in a convenient part of the city."

"That would ruin any desire to go take in a film on the big screen," I said.

"Or, any of the pro wrestling pay-per-view events that we sometimes go to together," the roommate added. "Speaking of which, those get out late, like close to 11 p.m. on a Sunday night. Would the buses in London be running that late? Because you wouldn't have the benefit of having Dennis swinging by from Richmond Hill – or wherever he ends up after his marriage gets flushed down the toilet – to drive you back and forth between your new apartment and the theatre."

Phil was fighting to defend his decision, but was beginning to lose the battle. "That is a very valid point, but I'm committed to my decision. And even then, my relocation wouldn't be for upwards of another year. There are certain conditions that need to be met on both of our ends before I actually start packing things up here."

I was curious, "What kind of conditions?"

"Well, we both have to build up a certain level of savings before we can afford first and last month's rent. Then, there's the cost of renting a truck, and hiring the movers to get all of my things down the 401; although, Amy said she might be able to convince her mother to help us out there. Plus, there's also the cost of any new furniture and appliances we may need once we get settled. It would be a costly venture, but if we both cut back on unnecessary expenditures between now and then, we might be able to pull it off."

I scratched my chin. "I see, and how exactly is Amy going to fund her end of the bargain? She's not expecting you to foot the entire bill here, is she?"

"Oh, no. One of the conditions I instituted was the requirement that she would submit an application for and get approved for proper social assistance. Sure, she gets some now through a couple of avenues, but it's definitely not enough to cover all of the monthly expenditures of living on her own, or in this case, with someone else."

Jim interjected again, "That seems sensible and all, but there is one thing you have to ask yourself at the end of the day: do you actually love Amy? Living together is a very big step in any relationship. But, if the two of you can't see yourselves as a couple for the long haul, then what is the point of going through all of this in the first place?"

If there was a question that would stop Phil's Moving Train dead in its tracks, his roommate had just thrown it on the table. It was the type of question that should be asked of any couple should they ever consider 'shacking up' with one another. How could two people in a relationship co-exist under the same roof if there was no mutual admiration between them? I looked at my friend, and I could finally see the same expression on his face that Karen reportedly had seen when he informed Jessica and I of his initial decision; a look of hollow conviction.

"You know what? I don't think I do. It's funny, though. When Amy asked me to take her back, I was cautious to begin with because I had not gotten back together with anyone I had been in a relationship with in close to 25 years. Yet, I decided to take a chance and reunite with her."

"Yes, you mentioned the two of you patched things up. When exactly did that happen?"

"It was about a week after we did the research interview for the novel I've been working on for this month. Amy invited me down for a weekend to take in the London version of that event Toronto holds every year where they open up different private buildings to the public for free tours."

"Ah yes, I know the event you speak of."

"Anyway, the first night that I was there, she told me she saw the error of her ways in the months after we broke up, and came to the realization that she liked being with me. So, she proposed that the two of us reform our relationship."

Jim blinked, "'Came to the realization'? Somehow I'm guessing that means when she went to Ottawa after she was here for her art gallery trip in September, things didn't go too smoothly with the guy she was staying with, and came to terms with the fact that you're the only guy who could put up with her indecisiveness."

"A comment she had admitted herself when she made her suggestion, but realizing that I wasn't getting any younger, I decided to give it another shot. But, like I said, I wasn't feeling too confident with it. I mean, she had dumped me once before. What's not to say that a few months down the road, she might do it again? Then, once the weekend was over, that was when she dropped the bombshell and suggested the two of us move in together. She would get her own apartment in London, and have me co-inhabit with her."

I concluded, "Sounds to me like she was trying to dig her claws into you in hopes you wouldn't have second thoughts about re-entering the relationship."

"It does look that way when you think about it. Personally, I think she is desperate to get away from her current home life, and sees me as someone who could help provide an easy out."

Jim persisted, "But, I reiterate, if you don't love her, then why would you want to shift your life all the way down there when you don't believe things would last?"

"To be honest, I don't think she loves me either. I mean, she likes being with me -- cuddling, and other bouts of near intimacy -- that kind of stuff. But, I don't think she really has it in her to say those special three words. Sure, she can cite the fact that we're so far apart geographically, and don't 'see' each other on a regular basis, but that's her hang-up. In my case, when I was with her in the past, I had such deep emotional stirrings for her. This time around it's different; I don't feel the same way as I did before."

I summarized, "So, if you're not in love with her, and she's not in love with you, then why bother going through this whole charade of packing up all of your things, moving to an entirely different city to live with someone for an undetermined amount of time where you wouldn't be happy in the long run?"

"The detective's right, Phil. Also, what's not to say that after you move down there, six months down the road, she decides she's had enough of you, moves onto someone else, and decides she wants to go live with them? You'll be all alone in that apartment, or asked to move out. Where will you live if you're thrown out; still in London, with your family in Peterborough, or would you find your way back here?"

"Honestly, I don't know. My family in Peterborough has been bugging me to move down there even before I came to live with you. However, I know the lifestyles of that branch of my family tree, and I don't think it would be a 'safe environment' for me, given my 'issues' with problem gambling."

"What kind of lifestyle would that be?"

My friend explained to him the concerns he has regarding certain members and gambling: one member's emotional gambling to escape problems at home, another member's need to gamble to further their desires to acquire more frivolous merchandise, and the supreme coup de grace... a third member actually employed by the province in a gambling venue. Upon hearing that, Jim could understand why Phil would be so hesitant to relocate there; it might trigger a dangerous relapse beyond what I witnessed when Jessica and I picked the writer up outside of Greenwood a couple of months ago.

Phil concluded "So really, the only solution I'd have should it come to that is move back here, and there's no guarantee that you would still be living in this unit in the event I do return."

"That's true. I was having difficulties covering the rent and other expenses before you came here. Then again, I was in between jobs at the time, but all the same. There's no way I would be able to afford the rent all on my own. I was offered the option to move into a one-bedroom unit, but nowadays, the rent for that is about as much as what we're paying now for this two-bedroom unit."

"And the only reason we've been able to get it for that is because of your seniority in this building. I mean, shit, you said you had been living in this unit for 20 years before I took the smaller bedroom."

"Actually, I checked the lease the other day from when my dad, my brother and I moved in. I've been living here since 1984."

I worked out the numbers in my head, "That's 28 years; quite a long time to be living in the same apartment."

"I'll say. My grandmother and I lived together in my former building next door for close to 30 years, but that was spread out over 3 different units on various floors. 28 years in the same place is something you hear about families in houses doing, not hi-rise apartments."

"Regardless of all of that, I was on a road to ruin before you moved in. Not just the struggling to pay the rent, but – as much as I don't like to bring it up – the little incident I had two and a half years ago."

"You mean, your week-long issue with the bottle?"

"That's exactly what I'm referring to. I was going to drink myself into oblivion, but you stopped that. I was so dehydrated; I collapsed in the bathroom, and was knocked unconscious. You were the one who called the paramedics who rushed over here, and whisked me away to Sunnybrook where they kept me for three weeks; half of that in Critical Care."

"I still remember they had to tear the bathroom door off its hinges to get you out of there. I was worried to death about you for fear you had done more damage when you smacked the back of your head against the back wall of the shower."

"Well, it's because of you saving my life, I started to see the error of my ways. Since then, I've been clean and sober."

"That's good in the long run. So, Phil, I have to ask, knowing that you two have been there for each other, do you think you could break up the good friendship you and your roommate share? Not only that, if you're not here, what's not to say that Jim might have a similar episode sometime in the future, and you're not around to get him the help that he needed. No offence, Jim."

"None taken, Detective, but you're right. Look, Phil, I know you have a big heart, and you don't like to hurt others that you care about, but I would be absolutely lost without you around. While you might think Dennis is my best friend, in all honesty, you really are."

The writer had a solemn look on his face while he weighed everything that his roommate and I had discussed with him. The allure of starting fresh was something that appealed to him, but there was the factor where he would be living with a woman who he didn't feel the same emotional attachment that he once did before. He would be taking a huge risk in relocating two hours away, and would be unhappy in the process. If he were to stay in his current living situation, he wouldn't have to leave the already established support circle he had forged with not only me and Jessica, but with Jim, as well.

The writer sighed, "You know what, guys? After listening to what you two had to say, and I admit, you've both made a very strong argument, I've decided to reverse my decision. I'm going to stay here."

"I know this was a very difficult decision to make, but in the long run, I think it's the best one."

"I concur with the detective. You and I are not only roommates, but we're good friends, and I'd really hate for a woman to come between the two of us."

"I hear you, Jim." The two roommates gave each other a 'bro hug'. "If there's one thing I've learned over the years, it's that women come and go over the course of a lifetime, but true friends last forever, and that's something you and I share."

"I can definitely attest to that. But please, Phil, whatever you do, don't tell Jessica that, or she will chew my ass out worse than what Lt. Davies did earlier this week."

Phil laughed, "Don't worry, Gary. Your secret is safe with me."

The two of us carefully toasted each other with our cooled cups of coffee, while we shared the box of doughnut holes with Jim. But, as we were enjoying our company, I realized there was one little piece of information I was left out of in the aftermath of bringing our culprit in for booking.

"You know, Phil, in all of the necessary procedural stuff in locking Stevens up, I didn't find out who won the professional Championship game tonight. What was the outcome?"

The look on my friend's face soured at the thought of the result, and I was given a slight inkling as what it was.

"Uh oh, given the expression you're giving me I'm guessing Toronto is celebrating a sixteenth title?"

Jim nodded, "That they are. They beat Calgary by 13 points. The Westerners couldn't even score a touchdown until late in the game."

"Calgary took way too many penalties, and it cost them dearly," Phil added. "I was hoping they would stick it to the Boatmen, but I guess they couldn't get the job done."

I chuckled, "All the more incentive next season for your Ti-Cats to prove to the league that the Double Blue was a one-year flash in the pan."

Jim replied, "Not just the Ti-Cats, but the other six teams in the league, as well."

"I know," Phil nodded. "But confidentially, I would so love for Hamilton to open up their new stadium in 2014 hoisting the Championship banner from Regina."

The three of us all laughed, and just sat in Phil and Jim's living room, chatting about Canadian football, the current state of professional hockey with its ongoing labour dispute, local politics – which involved the upcoming court decision about the mayor's conflict of interest case that he would eventually lose, and just about life in general. It was rare for me to have the opportunity to bond with many males in my life; most of them were fellow officers down at the Division. However, on this particular evening, I was enjoying the camaraderie that the best male friend I've ever had since Rob was gunned down, his roommate of the past five years, and yours truly experienced.

While I knew my two fellow conversationalists couldn't see her, I could feel the reassuring hand of my dearly departed fiancée on my shoulder. She mentioned how this was remarkable progress for me in expanding my social circle, and this was something that should be shared with not only my therapist down at the Division, but also the special woman in my life that is amongst the living. Jessica was right that it was probably for the best that I came to this Scarborough apartment alone. It provided the chance for me to have some proper male bonding time that I sorely lacked.

After chatting for about an hour, I left the apartment, as Jim mentioned that he had to get some sleep in advance of his morning shift at his workplace. Phil wanted to get some more writing in before he turned in for the night. I gave them both my regards, and suggested the three of us should meet up again, and see how we were faring. I made it back downstairs, climbed into my car, and drove home with the sense of my life being a little more whole than it was before.